Acc. No. 14 15. G

GW01081164

BAR KOCHBA

BAR KOCHBA

—————— • ——————

Amram Whiteman

—————— • ——————

BLOCH PUBLISHING CO., INC.
New York

Libray of Congress Catalogue Number 85-071323

ISBN 0-8197-0499-7

Printed in the United States of America.

For Donna, Coleman and Stanley

Chapter One

The year was 130 A.D., and a great and terrible rumor spread among the people of Jerusalem like a plague. Emperor Hadrian, in Rome, was thinking of rebuilding the whole city—making it a Roman city instead of a Jewish one! No one knew the details of the plan, but few shrank from making guesses. Rabbi Akiba, heavy with years and considered the wisest elder in all Judea, went about calming the people and assuring them that these were merely childish fancies which should be ignored and allowed to die a quick death. But one evening Aquila, Hadrian's closest aide and a former student of Akiba's, visited the Rabbi at his home in the northern part of Jerusalem. The old man, looking at Aquila's face, sensed immediately that beneath all the reports and idle whisperings was a kernel of truth.

"I bring bad news, Rabbi," were almost the first words from Aquila's lips.

"Sit down, sit down, my son," Akiba invited him with a gesture to a chair. "Rachel!" he called to his wife. "Wine for our guest."

Rachel, a little old lady with a very kind face, came out of the next room. Her eyes lit up when she saw Aquila.

"A guest indeed!" she cried. "But one who doesn't visit us often enough," she half–scolded him.

Aquila sat down, deeply warmed by the welcome. In a few moments he was sipping the wine Rachel had brought him and trying to steel himself to deliver his message.

"Yes, I would like to see you both more often," he answered. "But these days my work for Hadrian keeps me so busy that I have little time for anyting else. In fact even *this* visit has something to do with my duties."

Akiba's expression became serious.

"Aquila," he said, "we have been hearing things. It is all I can do to keep our people from doing something rash and foolish against the Roman soldiers who patrol our streets. Tell me. Is Hadrian planning some outrage against us?"

Aquila swallowed and then nodded.

"Yes, an outrage," he admitted.

His worst fears confirmed, the Rabbi demanded huskily, "What is it? What *is* it?"

"He—he wants to remove all our temples and put up Roman temples in their place!" the other blurted, feeling like a schoolboy in the presence of his teacher.

Akiba stood up, trembling. He turned around slowly and looked at his wife, who was still standing.

"Did you hear that, Rachel?" he asked faintly, his hand seeking the table for support.

She moved toward him concernedly.

"Rabbi!"

He turned back to the visitor, his mouth tightening.

"And you—what have *you* to do with all of this?"

Aquila's lips tried to form the words, but for a few moments they would not come out. At last he murmured, "*I* have been chosen to carry out his orders."

". . . And is this—is this what you came here tonight to tell me?"

The other looked up at him, playing with his cup nervously and pleading with his eyes to be understood.

"Rabbi, can't you see my position? I am Hadrian's aide. I *must* obey!"

"Must you?" was the indifferent reply.

Aquila stood up too.

"What would you have me do? Let him banish me—perhaps execute me?"

"Banishment isn't the worst fate for a man."

"He may go further! I can't predict his decisions."

Akiba stared at him.

"You *are* afraid of him, aren't you?"

"And you, Rabbi—you are not?"

"I fear only God."

"Rabbi—" Rachel interrupted, and paused.

He turned to her again.

"Yes?"

"I don't like to see you quarreling, you two who have always been so close together. Perhaps if—"

But he raised his hand with dignity, and she stopped.

"We are not quarreling," he said more mildly. "We are merely discussing this new crisis which faces us." A new idea struck him suddenly, and he said to Aquila, "I hear you are a good friend of Hadrian's, as well as his aide."

"What are you thinking of, Rabbi?"

"Why don't you talk to him again? Since you are now one of us, I believe you understand us very well. You can explain to him how strongly we feel about our temples. It may be that you can persuade him—" He paused, for the other was shaking his head and smiling sadly.

"I am afraid you don't know our emperor very well. To himself, he is something like a god who is never wrong. Why, if I came to him with such an idea as you suggest, he would—he would just laugh in my face!"

"Laugh in your face," Akiba repeated bitterly. "If a subject people were to ask for understanding, he would laugh in its face." He sat down suddenly, a picture of deep despair. Rachel put her hand on his shoulder consolingly. "There must be a way to solve this," he said, his hopes rising again. "There must!"

"It would take a miracle," said Aquila. "All we Jews can do is accept the edict and worship in our own homes."

"This may not be the end. Hadrian may go on to other things."

"Such as?"

Akiba shrugged.

"Who knows? I dare not imagine what evil schemes can enter the mind of a tyrant." A shadow crossed his face. "Perhaps he will even—" He stopped.

"What, Rabbi?"

Akiba shook his head.

"I cannot bring myself even to mention it. Let us pray that God will bring him to his senses and that he will not touch our temples."

Aquila bowed his head.

"The work begins in a few days."

The other looked up at him.

"In a few days?"

"I can delay it no longer. If this is any comfort to you, I shall begin not by tearing down Jewish temples, but by raising a temple to Jupiter on the site of our Second Temple, destroyed sixty years ago. Those are my orders. But afterward, our holy places must be wrecked too. I say this all at once, so that you may know exactly what we are facing."

Akiba stood up, Rachel's hand dropping from his shoulder.

"You will do all this, and still consider yourself one of us?"

"Rabbi," the other pleaded, "I must do as I'm told. Can't you see that?"

"If I were you, I'd rather die than carry out such orders." His face reddening, he pointed to the door. "Leave my house!"

"Rabbi," Rachel cried out, "Aquila is a friend. He is doing what he can for us!"

"It is not enough. He might as well be an enemy."

Aquila finally brought himself to speak.

"Is—is this your last word?"

"My last!"

The aide turned slowly and went out of the house.

"You were wrong, Rabbi!" said Rachel in tears. "You can't expect him to give up his life for us."

He stared at the door for a few moments.

"He was a good student," he murmured. "One of the best students I have ever had."

"And you ordered him out of the house as if he were a—an enemy!"

He looked at her.

"Rachel," he said evenly, "these are times when more is required than being a good student. Courage is needed. Self-sacrifice!" He closed his eyes, his lips moving in silent prayer. She lowered her head, accepting his judgment.

Chapter Two

Next morning Simon bar Koziba, a sandal maker of about thirty, was hard at work as usual in his shop near the heart of Jerusalem. He was tall and very muscular—in fact famous throughout the city for his feats of strength. One of his favorite tricks, for example, was to hold two full-grown men aloft, each balanced on one hand. But he rarely did this unless coaxed for a long time, for he felt that it was the power of the spirit which was important—not the power of the body.

An elderly neighbor, Daniel, entered, and the two men greeted each other cordially. Simon handed him his sandals, and Daniel, examining them, remarked, "Have you heard what people are saying?"

The shopkeeper grinned—a wide, infectious kind of grin.

"About me?"

But the customer did not smile back.

"No—about Hadrian."

Simon shrugged.

"I never listen to rumors."

The other, satisfied with his purchase, put the sandals

into a basket woven from palm leaves and paid Simon, saying at the same time, "I think it's going to be more than a rumor this time."

"*What* is?" asked Simon patiently.

"He has plans."

"Plans?"

"To rebuild Jerusalem."

"For what reason?"

Daniel shrugged too.

"He's the Emperor. He doesn't have to have reasons." And he moved to the door.

"Daniel!" Simon called, stopping him. But he changed his mind and broke into a laugh. "Never mind."

"You don't believe it, do you?"

"No, of course not."

"Well, *I* do!" said Daniel forcefully. "He's going to tear down our temples and put up Roman buildings and statues in their place!"

Simon shook his head.

"We Jews would never stand for it."

At that moment a patrol on horseback clattered by outside. Daniel waited till the sound of the hoofs had died away and then looked meaningfully after the soldiers.

"Stand for it? I guess we'll have to." He opened his basket for a moment and gave a final, approving look at the sandals. "Good job, Simon!"

"Thank you."

The customer left. Still thinking about the rumor, Simon returned to his work. He seemed worried for a few moments, but then suddenly broke into his open, attractive laugh again.

"Rumors!" he exclaimed aloud, although there was

no one in the shop. Only a fool paid any attention to them, he was sure.

In the evening he closed shop and returned home to have dinner with his wife, Leah, and ten-year-old son, Rufus. As soon as he sat down at the table, he thought of referring to what Daniel had said, but decided to wait till a bit later. He didn't want to worry either of them, and it would be a more pleasant meal if they talked of gayer things. Yet, as it turned out, it was Leah who first brought up the subject, just when they were about half through.

"I respect Hadrian," he told her. "He is a very learned scholar in both Greek and Roman literature. I can't understand how a man like that can do something as barbarous as to—"

"Learned or not, he is still a Roman emperor," she broke in heatedly, "ruling us as a subject people when we should be free, as we were in the old days!"

He studied her, Rufus looking a bit frightened.

"You believe, then, that he will dare to destroy our holy places?" Simon asked.

"What do *you* believe?"

"I think this whole thing is just an old wives' tale, and that we should go on enjoying our dinner as if that is exactly what it is, and no more!" He felt himself beginning to sweat a little between his shoulder blades under his warm, brown tunic, and tried to calm himself by smiling at her and going on, "Please, Leah, we're spoiling a lovely evening, getting excited about nothing at all."

Rufus suddenly scolded Leah, "Yes, don't get excited!"

At that both his parents burst into laughter, for Rufus had never talked that way to her before. She put her hand softly on his forehead and smoothed the frown away.

"All right, I'll do just as you say."

He grinned and returned to his tasty roast lamb with renewed appetite. Nothing more was said about the matter for the rest of the meal. Instead Simon asked his son a few questions about his school lessons, and was satisfied with the replies. "A bright boy," he thought proudly. "He'll go far."

After dinner he lay down on his bed for a few minutes, as was his custom, his arms folded under his head. The events of the day passed hazily through his mind and he closed his eyes sleepily. Tomorrow Ezekiel, an especially finicky customer, would be in his store asking—

"Simon!"

He opened his eyes again, and there was Leah standing over him concernedly.

"Don't forget about the Academy," she reminded him.

He started up, raising himself on his elbow.

"Oh, yes! The Acad—"

But she pushed him back gently. "Don't worry—I'll wake you up in time, if you fall asleep."

"Thank you," His head on the pillow again, he closed his eyes once more. No, he mustn't miss the Academy, as he had last week. Besides, tonight Rabbi Akiba would be there, and his was one lecture only a fool would want to sleep through.

An hour later Simon was sitting in the back of the main hall of the school, which he attended once a week. As usual, the large room was crowded with eager students —young people as well as adults. He looked about him. What excitement enlivened those many faces! The Rabbi was not there yet, but he was never late, and as the time for his appearance grew near, Simon could feel the suspense becoming keener and keener, almost as if it were a physical thing you could reach out and touch. At last, prompt as ever, the old man came in by a side entrance and stepped spryly, even cheerfully, to the platform. He was eighty years old, and yet somehow the youngest in the room. Everybody got up immediately and stood for a few moments in silent tribute to the greatest sage in Judea. He scanned the audience kindly, like a father, and then nodded—a signal for it to sit down as one man. Simon leaned forward to hear his first words, but this was wholly unnecessary, for they came out clear and firm.

"The Bible tells us," he began, and for an hour, which passed like five minutes, he explained and interpreted the Law. No one uttered a sound until he finished, smiled and asked in a somewhat less formal and more intimate tone, "Are there any questions?"

Yes, there certainly were. They opened in a trickle but soon flooded the room like a river. Simon had one, but each time he raised his hand there seemed to be a dozen others, springing up like a sudden forest, and equally demanding of the Rabbi's attention, and so he was never called on. Then a very worried person mentioned the rumor about Hadrian's plans, and instantly, as if by prearrangement, the entire hall was quiet, except for a fifteen-year-old boy near Simon who sucked in his breath with a loud, excited, rather funny sound which everybody understood and could really not blame him for.

Akiba's expression changed. He said nothing for a few seconds, but gravely wet his upper lip with his tongue, preparing to answer. Simon, studying his eyes from his seat in the rear, noticed a multitude of variations in the light shining from them, as if each thought behind them had its own particular kind of look. Then the answer came at last, measured and thoughtful:

"I have been meaning to tell you, and I am glad you asked me. Aquila visited me the other evening."

"Aquila!" was the whisper of many voices.

"Yes—Hadrian's aide and adviser, and, since about a year ago, a Jew and a lover of Jewish lore. But the news he brought me from the Emperor was sad. This rumor you refer to—" His voice had become suddenly husky for the first time, and he stopped to clear it.

"Go on!" a heavy-set man burst out with angry impatience. The explosion seemed so impudent and out of place in that dignified gathering that those near him turned on him with such outraged cries as, "Wait, can't you?", "Shame on you!" and "Show some respect!" Abashed, the poor fellow sank low in his seat and said nothing else for the rest of the evening.

But the Rabbi smiled understandingly at him.

"Yes, I'll be glad to." His voice was resonant and controlled again. "The rumor is well-founded, it seems." His face became grave again as he turned back to the whole audience. "Aquila has been given the assignment of rebuilding Jerusalem—making it into a Roman city instead of a Jewish one." A gasp of horror and hatred spread through the hall, but before anyone could say a word, he continued, "All our temples are to be torn down, and Roman shrines will be put up in their place. The work may begin any day—perhaps even tomorrow."

Simon had a foolish but almost irresistible impulse to jump to his feet and shout, "And what are we going to *do* about it?" But something held him to his chair like a strong, invisible hand. How could he presume to use

such a tone to a great Rabbi? Surely the speaker needed
no prompting from anybody, but would tell them what
must now be done without any of them having to remind
him. So Simon wisely held his peace.

Yet the Rabbi remained silent, obviously waiting for
someone else to say something. At last Michael, a pious
and elderly man who had never been known to miss a
lecture at the Academy, pleaded, "Rabbi! What are we
going to do?"

This was all the rest needed. In a single moment the
entire room was filled with a roar of mingled protest,
indignation and anguish. Simon could not hear a word,
and he even had to cover his ears with the palms of
his hands to shut out the din. But when Akiba raised
his hand, the noise died away as quickly as it had begun.

"We can only pray that Hadrian will change his mind,"
he said solemnly. He closed his eyes and lifted his face
a little, his lips moving in an inaudible plea for God's
mercy. A few in the audience closed their eyes too, and
soon there was nothing except the faint, fervent hum of
prayers, each slightly different from the other, but all
addressed to the Creator and asking for help in a time
of great crisis. Yet there was one man who prayed not at
all, He sat like a stone until the last of the others had
poured out his heart and was finished.

"Prayers!" he cried out suddenly. "Yes, prayers are all
very well, but what shall we do if the Emperor does *not*
change his mind? What if our holy city is turned into a
Roman city? Shall we smile and thank the imperial Hadrian for making our ugly little town beautiful?"

Stunned, the others said nothing. Akiba looked at this
man calmly and then spoke:

"Let us first see whether our prayers are answered, Joseph. But if it happens that God in His wisdom permits Hadrian—" He stopped. For the second time his voice had become husky, and his whole body wavered till it seemed he might even fall. A young man seated directly in front of him rushed up to support him, but he turned to him with a smile and held him off. "Thank you, my son. I—I am all right now." Indeed, he straightened, appeared himself again, and the youth returned to his seat. "If God in His wisdom permits our holy places to be desecrated," he went on resolutely, "we must resist the Emperor! Yes, with arms, if necessary! For after all, to us Jews our faith is as important as our life—*is* our life —and demands every sacrifice." He paused again and turned back to Joseph.

"Are you answered now, my friend?"

"Yes, Rabbi," said the other much more humbly. "I'm —sorry if I sounded disrespectful."

Again Simon wanted to speak, and this time it was as if that firm, unseen hand had closed over his mouth. "Arms, yes!" he had wanted to shout. "But who will lead us? You, Rabbi? Hadrian would crush us in a day." The air in that hall seemed suddenly to stifle him, and he got up and almost ran out into the street, leaving some of the men he nearly stumbled over murmuring about the bad manners of some people. Once outside, he breathed in the cold clear air deeply and felt better. He looked up at the sky. Those countless stars! They seemed so distant, so indifferent. Did *they* care about Hadrian? Rebuilding Jerusalem? The threat of a revolt? Perhaps God was like the stars. He trudged home through the dark streets. As he came nearer his house, he was startled by what sounded like the screams of a boy.

Chapter Three

He ran in the direction of the screams and soon saw what was happening. A big, powerful Roman soldier had a boy of about eleven by the neck and was cuffing him about violently. Simon hurried closer and demanded, "What's the matter? What has he done?"

But the soldier, instead of answering, glared at him for a moment, thrust the boy aside and pushed Simon to the ground. Simon, his head still full of resentful thoughts about what he had heard this evening and in no mood to be mistreated by *any*body, let alone a Roman patrolman, leaped to his feet in an instant and hurled himself at his throat. Surprised by this counterattack, the soldier fell flat on his back, his skull hitting a broken jar which had been left carelessly in the street. For a few seconds he seemed dazed, but then, as the sandal maker's strong fingers closed doggedly on his throat, he began to wriggle and gasp in a deadly struggle to be free of his sudden enemy. Wildly and furiously Simon continued to tighten his grip on the yielding flesh, as if the only purpose he had been created for was to dispose then and there of this monster, this sign and symbol of everything he hated. Somewhere in the corner of his mind he heard the boy scuttling down the street in terror. When the soldier's gasps became huskier and more frantic and his eyes grew glassy, something stopped Simon's fingers and he withdrew them slowly, staring at the now unconscious man as if the whole thing were a dream. What was he doing in that street? What had happened? Suddenly he remembered it all very clearly, and he jumped to his feet again. It was a madness which had seized him, born of years of loathing the Roman invaders of his beloved Jerusalem. He looked at his hands. Didn't he remember his own strength? Why, in another few seconds the Roman would surely have been dead. He heard footsteps, and darted into the doorway of a building. They receded, the unconscious figure unnoticed, and Simon made his way quickly home.

At his door he hesitated, inspecting his tunic. There were rips here and there where his victim had clutched at him in his agony, and there was also some blood where his nails had dug in. Again there were footsteps, and Simon opened the door swiftly and entered, closing it behind him. No point in being seen by anybody, Jew or Roman! Leah was sitting at the table, and glanced up. She covered her mouth with her hand in an abrupt, horrified movement, as if to suppress an outcry. But after a moment she could not restrain herself and exclaimed, "Simon!"

"Don't be alarmed," he assured her as he approached. "I'm all right. I—I was in a fight with a Roman. He was pushing one of our boys around, and I—I guess I saw red. I almost killed him." He sat down next to her and tried to catch his breath, realizing for the first time just how tired he was.

"Where is he now?" she asked fearfully, putting her arm around his shoulders.

He stared at her, gathering his wits.

"The Roman? Still there, I guess—where I left him."

"In the street?"

"Yes."

She took away her arm, covered her face with her hands and began moaning.

"Oh, Simon!"

"Don't be afraid. I just won't go to the shop for a few days, and we'll see what happens." He looked around. "Where's Rufus?"

"Asleep already."

"Good. Let's not tell him anything about this." And he sighed.

"What's the matter?"

"That boy in the street—he looked so much like Rufus, although he was a little older. When I saw that big, husky Roman—" He stopped, nearly tearful with renewed rage, and clenched his fist. She put her hand over it sympathetically.

"I understand." An anxious new thought occurred to her, and she demanded, "Do you think either of them will recognize you again?"

He shook his head. "I don't think so. There was a moon, but luckily for me it was hidden by clouds. We fought in the dark."

"But Simon," she asked plaintively, "couldn't you have just—argued with him? Did you have to—"

"Argue!" he interrupted grimly, and so loudly she was sure Rufus would wake up. "I tried to, but didn't get a single word out of him. All he did was push me to the ground!"

She stood up.

"And that's when you—attacked him," she said, look-ing down at him.

He raised his head, returning her look and wondering what she was getting at.

"Yes . . ." He added, with sudden sharpness, "Why, what *should* I have done? Thanked him for his trouble?"

"But see the trouble you're in now! Why, you can't even go to work. They'll hunt for you—" She stopped, covering her face with her hands again. He stood up too and held her tightly against him.

"Don't worry," he said in a lower tone as he remem-bered Rufus. "Those Romans don't really care very much even about each other. It's only we Jews who con-sider human life holy. My guess is that in a few days they'll forget about this whole thing!" he finished cheer-fully.

She stared at him.

"You really think so?"

He nodded vigorously, smiling.

Her eyes dropped, and once more she noticed the bloodstains and the rents in his tunic. She touched his left sleeve, which had an especially ugly rip. "Anyway," she went on, sounding much more like her usual self, "take this off right away and we'll burn it. You'll need a bath too."

He glanced at the door and remembered that a Roman soldier might come knocking at any moment, and there he stood, with all the evidence of the attack on him. Quickly he followed her advice and removed his tunic.

For the next few days he stayed away from his shop. When Rufus came home the first day and found him there, he asked Leah why, and she explained, "Your father isn't feeling well today, and decided to stay home.

He may be here for a few days until he is better again."
Although he was worried about Simon's health, the boy
asked no further questions.

One afternoon, when Rufus was still at school, Leah
came in breathlessly with news she had heard in the
market. The Romans were making a house-to-house
search for the thug who had assaulted the soldier! Simon
gripped her arms.

"Leah, it's something we rather expected, so let's take
it calmly."

"But you were hoping they wouldn't, weren't you?
Didn't you say that night you came home—"

"I remember what I said!" he interrupted. "But you
can't always be absolutely sure about these things." He
turned away from her for a few moments as he thought
as hard as he could about what needed to be done now.

"Maybe you ought to try to leave Jerusalem immediately!" she suggested shrilly, and he saw that he hadn't
succeeded at all in getting her to accept the situation.
Very close to losing his temper, he almost pushed her
into a nearby chair.

"Leah! You mustn't be so frightened. That's exactly
what the Romans would have us all be—so scared we
don't know what we're doing, and play easily into their
hands. Don't you see that?"

She nodded.

"Yes." And she went on agitatedly, "But what can I
do? I am only a woman, and I *am* frightened!"

He seized her shoulders and was sorely tempted to
shake her, but at the very last moment removed his
hands.

"Yes, you are a woman," he said kindly. "Perhaps I'm
expecting too much. Still, if a Roman came to our door

this very minute, it's very important that you behave as if nothing were wrong, or else he'd become suspicious and start poking around far more than he would otherwise. Why, you'd just be giving me away! Can't you understand that?" he pleaded.

"Yes, of course. My mind does, but my feelings . . ."

He smiled.

"They're running away with you, and that's a big mistake."

More than anything else, it was his smile which quieted her a little. At least, she was gratefully aware, her heart didn't pound quite so heavily against her chest any more. She even managed to smile back.

"You're behaving as if this is all something of a joke," she remarked.

He shrugged.

"Our lives are in the hands of the Lord. If He wishes to take mine, there is nothing I can do to prevent Him."

"Will you leave Jerusalem?" she asked, remembering her own suggestion.

He shook his head.

"No."

"Why not?"

He leaned down close to her and patted her cheek, almost as if she were a child.

"Leah, where have you been? Have you ever taken a really good look at those gates? I'd have to pass through them, you know, on my way out."

"You mean the—the guards?"

"Yes, the guards, and I'm sure there are a few more of them now that the search is on. I wouldn't have a chance unless I flew over them. And in spite of my excellent physical condition, flying doesn't happen to be one of my talents!"

She thought intensely, biting her lip and raising her hand to her forehead.

"Maybe one of them could be bribed. I once heard of a case—"

He stopped her with a wave of his hand.

"Too risky. Besides, I'd have to bribe nearly all of them, and I'm not that rich."

"Not nearly all of them, Simon," she disagreed. "If—"

"Leah!" he almost snarled. She gave a hurt, startled cry, and he was instantly apologetic. "I'm sorry, but don't you see? We're wasting some very valuable time talking about something which can never happen. No, I'm not going to try to escape from town, because that would only be an open confession that I was the one who attacked the soldier. Right now they don't know anything." He heard shouts in the street and stopped. There was another shout, and he urged Leah, "Go see what it is."

She stood up, walked slowly to the door, opened it and looked out. She stared for a few seconds, closed it quickly and turned back to him.

"It's the Romans! They're right on this street."

"The searchers."

"Yes!"

Eyeing her directly, he approached and took hold of her shoulders again.

"Now remember what I told you. Above everything else, try to be calm, or in a frightened moment you'll make them suspicious and only give me away." As she didn't answer, he pressed her, "Are you all right?"

There was a knock on the door.

"Open!" came the command, loud and rough.

"I'm all right," she nodded, and turned bravely to obey.

Chapter Four

There were three of them, and they were in a hurry. One of them, who seemed to be in charge, glanced at Leah and brushed her aside. Simon made an instinctive movement toward her, for he could not endure seeing her treated roughly, but she looked at him, and there was no misreading the message in her eyes: "Please be careful!" And so he stood his ground grimly and waited.

The Roman, a centurion (commander of 100 men), was a burly fellow with a craggy sort of face which made it very clear he meant business. He glared at Simon from head to foot, strode over and planted himself arrogantly in front of him, his hands on his waist and his feet spread apart.

"Who are you?" he demanded.

"Simon bar Koziba."

Unexpectedly, the Roman's expression relaxed into a smile, and he stepped back a little as if to see him better.

"Oh, yes, I've heard of you! The Jewish strong man."

"God gave me a strong body," Simon answered humbly.

"God?"

"Our God," he repeated firmly.

The soldier studied Simon's hands for a few moments, and then turned to the others.

"See those hands! He could strangle an ox."

They saw, and nodded appreciatively.

"I never saw anything like them," one remarked, adding with a chuckle, "we could use a fellow like that."

"Gentlemen," Simon interjected, "I am sure you did not come here in the middle of the afternoon to discuss my strength. My wife and I would be very grateful to you if—"

"Silence!" roared the centurion, his mood changing instantly. "We know exactly what we are after, and who are you to tell us our business?"

Simon felt his face reddening with anger, but another pleading look from Leah made him force himself to be calm. To think he had been worried about the way *she* would act!

"I—I'm sorry," he heard himself say as if another man were speaking.

"What are you doing here in the middle of the afternoon anyway?" the officer went on. "Are you sick?"

"Yes, he's sick." Leah put in quickly.

The soldier glared at him up and down again, smiling doubtfully.

"I've never seen a healthier–looking specimen in my whole life."

"He should be in bed right now!" she protested. "He got up when we heard—shouts in the street."

"Let him speak for himself!" he ordered, scowling.

"I'm sorry."

Simon, deciding to play a convincing role, put his

hand dazedly to his forehead and moved toward the bedroom.

"Where are you going?" the centurion demanded harshly.

"I—I'm not feeling well. I have a very bad headache, and I'm afraid I also have the fever. Will you excuse me?"

"No!"

Simon stopped and faced him again, swaying uncertainly.

"Would you have me fall to the floor to prove I am ill?"

The other darted forward suddenly and pointed to a rather deep scratch, still healing, on Simon's right forearm where the patrolman had clutched at him in his agony of choking.

"How did you get this?" he demanded.

Simon hesitated only a second, his brain racing.

"I am a sandal maker by trade," he explained smoothly. "One of the tools I use—"

"Enough! Of course you would have an excuse. Do you know why we're making this search?"

"Yes."

"If we don't find—" He stopped abruptly, whispered something to the other soldiers and turned back to him.

"Stay here for the next few hours," he advised. "We're a little suspicious of you, but not enough to make us want to take you along with us. Do you understand?"

"Yes, sir."

"We may be here later, or we may not. But if we are, and you're gone, I promise you we will search for you in every corner of Jerusalem, and when we find you, we *will* take you with us! Have I made myself clear?"

"Very clear, sir."

At that moment the door opened and Rufus came in, returning from school. When he saw the soldiers, he made as if to run, but Simon called after him, "Rufus!" The boy came back slowly, stood beside him and received a little protective hug.

"Don't be afraid," Simon assured him. "These soldiers are just doing their duty, searching for someone, but they know I'm not their man."

Rufus, too frightened to say anything, stared at them.

"Is this your son?" asked the centurion.

"Yes."

He took a step forward and leaned down, about to ask him something, but then changed his mind. Straightening, he walked to the door, stood stiffly and thoughtfully for a few moments, and marched out decisively, the others following in good military order. At last the door was closed. None of the three remaining in the room dared even breathe until they heard the heavy footsteps receding down the street to the next house. Then Leah rushed into her husband's arms, and he embraced both her and the boy warmly.

"They'll be back!" she moaned. "They said they'd be back!"

"They said they might or they might not," he corrected her gently, patting her shoulder.

"Will you stay here and wait? Perhaps it would be better if—"

"I'll wait!" he interrupted. "They have no reason to suspect me, except for—" He looked regretfully at the scratch on his forearm. "If only I had thought of wearing something to cover that!"

"It's not too late to put another tunic on," she said, and went into the next room to get one for him.

The next three or four hours were very suspenseful, but when the sun had set and there was still no sign of returning soldiers, Simon and Leah began to hope that their suspicions had not been strong enough to make them want to come back for a further check. Perhaps they had discovered a few who aroused their doubts more than the "Jewish strong man" and were concentrating on them. At any rate Simon relaxed and even made a few jokes, which Leah enjoyed. Rufus found his tongue at last and laughed as heartily as his parents. And yet, lying in bed that night and trying to fall asleep, Simon could not help worrying about what the next day would bring. For that was the day he had planned to go back to work.

Early the next morning he left his house and walked the short distance to his shop. He opened the door, stepped in briskly and looked around, half expecting to see some changes made in his absence, but of course, since he had no assistants and the store had been bolted against intruders for days, there were none. He began to busy himself with work which was long overdue, and in an hour it seemed to him he had never been away.

Suddenly he heard shouts in the street. His first thought was that in these troubled times there appeared to be no end to these public outcries. He opened his door to see what was happening. Just across the street, in front of a large fruit market owned by Micah, a good customer of his, there had gathered a group of neighbors and fellow shopkeepers engaged in a very spirited discussion of a subject which he could not determine from where he stood. Every once in a while one of them would raise his voice, shouting, "Impossible!" or "They wouldn't *dare!*" or "We must do *some*thing!"

He closed his door behind him and darted across the

street to join them. For a few moments he could get no idea of what had happened until Micah turned to him.

"Simon!" he exclaimed. "Where have you been?"

"I've been sick. But what is all this about?"

"Are you all right now?"

"Never mind about my health!" he replied impatiently. "I'm fine." He gestured at the group. "What's happening?"

"*Two* things, as if one weren't enough. You know, of course, about the attack on the Roman soldier?"

"Yes, I've heard of it."

"Well, ten Jews have already been seized and are being held right now as hostages until the guilty one gives himself up!"

Simon's jaw tightened.

"They wouldn't dare!" he heard himself echoing one of the shouts.

"They're daring," Micah contradicted him. "What's more, Tinnius, our blessed governor, has publicly announced that if none of us comes forward to confess by noon tomorrow, the ten will surely die!"

Simon turned away, his face working. So *this* was what the outcry was about!

"And that's not all," Micah went on.

He faced him again.

"What more can there be?"

"Have you heard the rumor about Hadrian's rebuilding Jerusalem?"

"Yes, I have!" His expression had suddenly become so furious at the news he had already received that the other stood there open-mouthed a moment, wondering whether to continue at all. Angrily impatient, Simon seized him and demanded, "Is there anything more? Tell me without any of your old woman's gabble!"

"The—the work has already begun," Micah quavered, badly frightened. "The ruins of our sacred temple are already being cleared away to make room for a Temple of Jupiter." He clutched Simon's hands and tried to pull them away. "You're—you're hurting me."

Simon looked at them as if they were strangers to his will. "I'm sorry," he murmured, and dropped them to his sides. "I was carried away."

"It's terrible news," Micah nodded sympathetically.

By this time several of the others had approached them and were devouring every word.

"And do you know who is in charge of clearing the ruins?" a tall, gaunt man asked Simon.

"Yes, I heard it from Akiba the other evening at the Academy. Aquila."

"Yes, Aquila—one of us!" he exploded. "I told everybody two years ago, when it was being decided whether or not to accept him as a Jew, that he was not trustworthy, but no one would listen! 'A fine student,' the Rabbis said. 'A good man.' And now, when Hadrian just lifts his finger—"

"Enough!" Simon silenced him with a roar, and at the sound of it those who were still conversing by themselves stopped and drew near. "Our first problem is the hostages. Do you know exactly who they are?" he asked Micah.

"Yes!" Quickly he named them, and a sad roll call it was. When he finished, Simon looked around at the crowd, which had by now swelled to about fifty.

"Go about your business," he advised them. "I have work to do." As they began to move away doubtfully, he called after them, "Do not be afraid! Those hostages will be released." At this, several exchanged doubtful glances which he had no time to notice, for he turned quickly, crossed the street, bolted the door of his shop and made his way home, trying as hard as he could to conceive the very kindest and wisest way to break the news to Leah.

He hesitated at his door, for he was still puzzled as to what he ought to say.

Chapter Five

"Simon!" he heard her voice behind him. "Is anything wrong?"

He wheeled around.

"I thought you were inside."

"No, I've been doing a little shopping." As he glanced at her empty hands, she added with a smile, "That is, trying to. They didn't have exactly what I wanted."

"What did you want?"

"Simon!" she exclaimed, her smile disappearing. "It's not important. What *is* important is why you're home so early. Please tell me right away or I'll imagine the worst!"

He opened the door for her.

"Let's go in and I'll tell you there."

She obeyed, and he followed. When the door was closed behind them, she faced him again, her expression one of passionate entreaty, as if saying, "Please tell me what's happened, and don't make me ask you again!"

He lost no time explaining what had brought him home so soon. He gave her the news about the hostages, as well as the clearing away of the temple ruins.

She sat down, not answering but trying to decide what must be done. He moved closer to her.

"The first thing we must make up our minds about is, shall I give myself up?" he said.

She looked up at him, frightened.

"Of course you mustn't! How can you even *think* of it? They'll kill you at once!"

"But if I don't go to the Romans before noon tomorrow, ten innocent Jews will die. Would you prefer that?"

"Who are the hostages? Do we know any of them?"

"Yes, two—Joseph and Ezekiel." He frowned. "There is a third, but I'm not sure about him—I may be confusing him with someone else of the same name."

"Joseph and Ezekiel? I never heard of them."

"But I know them both, and well. They are fine fellows, both with families."

"Maybe this is just a bluff to terrify us all. They just want somebody to confess, but if nobody does, they may release the hostages after a prison term."

He shook his head.

"I don't think they're bluffing. Remember last year when—"

"Yes, I remember. The same kind of thing happened, nobody came forward, and they killed three hostages, didn't they?"

"And one a rabbi," he nodded, and raised his voice in a sudden outburst of anger. "They will stop at nothing! And then this new plan of Hadrian's—can you think of anything more barbaric? As if our own shrines were worthless, and only Roman buildings are important. He is trying to destroy our religion—that's what he's trying to do!"

She put her hand over his.

"Worry about our religion some other time, Simon. Your very life is at stake. What are we going to *do?*"

He stroked his beard thoughtfully.

"Akiba," he murmured.

"What?"

"Akiba—Rabbi Akiba!" he said more strongly, his face lighting up. "He is the wisest of us all. He will advise us!"

"Yes, the Rabbi!" she answered, her spirits rallying. "You're very close to him, aren't you?"

He hesitated, a bit embarrassed.

"I've listened to his lectures, but the fact is I've rarely actually spoken to him."

"Then why—"

"To tell you the truth," he admitted, "he is so brilliant I've always been afraid to say something foolish. I have been very happy just to listen. But this is no time," he went on grimly, "to lurk in the background like a shy little schoolboy! I must go to him right now!" He moved toward the door.

"Simon!" she called after him, getting up. He turned around. "I'm—I'm very frightened. He may tell you to give yourself up, and I'll never see you again!"

He came back to her and embraced her.

"No chance of that. If that is what he tells me to do, I'll return here first. Anyway I—I'd want to see Rufus again too. We'll have about twenty-four hours together." He dropped his hands, but she still held on to him, her head on his shoulder. "Please, Leah. I must go now—the time is so short." Slowly he drew her arms away from him, in spite of her resistance. But suddenly she clung to him more fiercely than ever, burying her tearful face in his shoulder. "Leah!" he cried out agonizedly. "We must have faith."

At last he was able to tear himself away, open the door and go down the street toward the Rabbi's home. Thoughts crowded his mind and troubled his heart. What if he had to give himself up to the Romans! Would they kill him immediately? After all, the man he had attacked still lived, or his death would have been part of the Roman announcement. It was only fair that—

He felt suddenly faint, and lurched to the wall of a building to steady himself. He looked around. What was happening? It wasn't such a hot day. Why, he wasn't even perspiring! And yet the dizziness came and went in waves. He straightened, shook his head vigorously and took his hand away from the wall. Why, he had never fainted in his life, and he wasn't going to break the habit of—

But determination wasn't enough, for the people he saw in the street seemed to grow hazy again, and if he hadn't reached out for that wall once more, he would surely have fallen. Then abruptly the wall itself seemed to turn to water, and he pitched forward on his face like a drunkard. At the very last moment he had the pres-ence of mind to raise his arm in front of him like a shield, so that only his chin was bruised a little. He slipped instantly into a state of unconsciousness, except that little sparks and colors scurried across his brain, and even a strange dream or two lingered there. Then there were no more colors and dreams—just a sound which made him roll over on his back, open his mouth and pant like a man who has run a great distance. It seemed that God was speaking to him. God Himself—just His voice —was speaking to him, giving him a message! Con-sciousness began to return, and he sensed he was listen-ing to God, and at the same time lying there in the street, somewhere between his own home and Rabbi Akiba's. The Voice faded away, but he knew that, sleeping or waking, he would never forget what it had said even if he lived to be a thousand years old.

He felt himself being propped up to a sitting position and at last opened his eyes. A man he had never seen before held him in his arms.

"Are you all right?" the stranger asked.

"Yes, I—I must have fainted." Simon rubbed his eyes, and when he opened them again, he looked around almost frantically, for the passerby had disappeared. He struggled to his feet and stood erect. His dizziness, like a storm which comes and goes quickly, now left him entirely. In fact he had never felt so clear-headed in his life! He began to walk down the street toward the Rabbi's house again, his steps firm. He could have danced!

Akiba lived in a simple house, very much like his own. No one would have suspected that it was the dwelling of the greatest sage in Israel. But then the Rabbi was famous for his humility, as well as for the simplicity of his tastes.

Simon knocked confidently on the door, for had not God spoken to him? What better way of introducing himself could there be, if the Rabbi did not recognize him immediately as a student of his?

Rachel, Akiba's wife, appeared.

"May I speak to the Rabbi?" he asked courteously.

"Of course." She led the way in. "Please sit down." He did so, and she left the room. In a few moments the Rabbi entered and Simon stood up again, but was immediately waved back into his chair. His host remained standing and studied him.

"Aren't you a student of mine?" he inquired at length.

"Yes, Rabbi," Simon replied, proud to be remembered. "My name is Simon."

"Ah, yes! Simon bar Koziba. You're married and have a child."

"Yes, sir." And he exclaimed inwardly, "What a memory!"

"And how may I help you, my son?" the other went on warmly.

Simon's expression became very serious. For several seconds he couldn't decide which of two matters he ought to discuss first—the Voice or his attack on the Roman. At last, when he noticed signs of impatience beginning to disturb his host's tranquil face, he plunged ahead, "God has just spoken to me, Rabbi! He has charged me with the mission of freeing the Jews from the tyranny of the Romans."

The Rabbi said nothing to this, his expression hardly changing.

"And that is not all, sir," Simon went on, breathing more freely now that at least part of his news had been unburdened. "I am the man who struck down the Roman patrolman."

Akiba answered after a few moments, "I see. Is there —anything else?"

"No, Rabbi. That is all."

Akiba drew up a chair slowly and sat down.

"I'm glad you came to me," he continued rather huskily. "To be very frank with you, I—I don't know which to talk to you about first: your—your message from God, or your—confession."

Simon nodded, smiling.

"I had the same trouble a minute ago. But then I decided the message would be the more important, since

it came from God, and the other is simply a police matter."

Akiba nodded back.

"A wise decision. We shall discuss these points, therefore, in the very logical order in which you brought them
up. First, the message. How exactly did it come to you?
Did God appear to you on the street and—"

"Yes, on the street!" Simon broke in, suddenly fever-
ish to tell the news, but he covered his mouth with his
hand just as suddenly. How could he have dared inter-
rupt the Rabbi? His own discourtesy shocked him.

But Akiba understood, and smiled reassuringly.

"Go on, my son. I am glad to see you are so very
anxious to tell me everything."

"Yes, I am! On my way here from my house I fell in
a faint—I, who have never fainted in my life!—and heard
a Voice—God's Voice—telling me what I must do."

"Did you—see Him at all?"

"No, there was—nothing. Only His Voice."

"In other words, it was a dream."

"Yes, a dream."

"Then how can you be sure it was really God's Voice,
and not just part of your dream?"

Simon hesitated, groping intensely for a way to express himself.

"I knew it!" he insisted at last. "I could just—feel it!
God spoke to me just as clearly as you're speaking to me
now."

"I see. Now what exactly did this—this Voice of yours
say? Can you remember His exact words?"

"Perfectly! He said, 'Simon bar Koziba, you are the
Messiah the Jews have been longing for. I am charging
you with the mission of freeing them from the Romans.'"

"And that was all? Just those few words?"

"Yes, that was all."

"Did you answer?"

"No, sir, I was too—frightened, I guess."

"And what happened after that? Did you have another dream?"

"No. I woke up. A—a stranger had raised me to a sitting position. He asked me if I was all right, but before I had much of a chance to reply and thank him, he was —gone."

"This—stranger, now; are you very sure you never saw him before?"

"Positive!"

The Rabbi looked at him closely for a few seconds and then stood up.

"Now about this confession," he said more sternly. "What made you attack the Roman?"

"He was—mistreating one of our boys."

"Mistreating? In what way?"

"He had him by the neck and was pushing him around. When I asked the Roman what the boy had done, he pushed *me* to the ground. Rabbi, I—it was too much. I jumped at him and almost strangled him."

"And now you are sorry?"

"Only because of the hostages!" he answered defiantly. "The brute deserved everything he got."

"I'm sure he did," the Rabbi nodded, sitting down again and reflecting. "Still . . ."

Simon waited for the decision, which he knew he must accept, whatever it might be, and he steeled himself for the worst. At last it came.

"I'm afraid you have placed me in a very difficult position. I shall give you my opinion, since you have come to me for it, and it is that our first concern must be for those hostages. After all, they are ten innocent men, and—"

Simon lifted his hand.

"I understand. You wish me to give myself up."

"Yes, immediately."

"And my—my dream?"

"Your dream," Akiba repeated.

"Yes! God spoke to me, didn't He? If I give myself up, how can I obey Him? He called me the—"

"Yes, I know. He called you the Messiah."

"And my mission is to—"

"To deliver us all from the Romans."

"You—you do not believe this! To you, this is just a foolish dream which I should try to forget as quickly as possible!" His tone changed from anguish to sad resignation. "The Romans will help me forget it."

"Simon, I am only a human being. I must pray for God's guidance in this, as in everything else of importance. I must also confer with the other rabbis, who will contribute their ideas, and pray too. Together we will arrive at our final decision. In the meantime, however . . ."

"I must place myself in the hands of the Romans."

Akiba stood up, walked to the door and opened it.

"You are free to go now," he said. "Free to return to your work and your home. Spend the next few hours with your family. Where do you live, in case I must see you again very soon?"

Simon gave him the exact location.

"Do just as you like," the other went on. "But remember my advice, for which you came of your own free will. Listen to your own heart, and see if it does not echo what I have told you."

"Thank you, Rabbi." He approached the door and hesitated there for a moment. "If I have sounded bitter and even disrespectful—"

"Not at all. Go with my blessing, my son. I know that whatever you do will be the right thing."

Simon walked down the street towards his home, the door closing behind him. So this is what he must do! Yes, of course. How could he had dreamed otherwise? Those ten innocent men—they must be saved, no matter what the cost.

And now there was Leah to break the news to. Even Rufus must know. He came to the street where he had fainted and looked about, half expecting to see the stranger again. And the message from God! Was that simply nonsense which he must now cast out of his mind forever like some idiot's fancy, and not even reveal to Leah? He glanced down at the exact spot where he had lain for a few minutes—or was it seconds? Then he moved on, the image of her taut, agonized face troubling him deeply. What harsh news to bring home to so loving a wife!

Chapter Six

Leah knew the Rabbi's decision even before Simon spoke—it was written so clearly in every line of his face, and in the way he tried to keep his eyes from her.

"He—he wants you to give yourself up, doesn't he?" she asked.

He looked at her, and then nodded grimly. Her mouth tightened with a growing determination. She took a step back.

"Don't do it!" she cried out in defiance. "You don't *have* to, do you?"

"No, Leah, I don't," he admitted. "He's left the matter entirely up to my own—conscience."

"I can tell by your expression," she answered, studying him. "You've made up your mind, haven't you? You're going to do just exactly as he says!"

"Leah, I must! Don't you see? There are ten innocent men who have every right—"

"Stop it!" she screamed, cupping her palms over her ears. "I don't want to hear one more word about those men!"

He came up to her, took her wrists and drew them firmly down to her sides. She stared up at him, wondering what he was going to say.

"You know I love you very much," he told her quietly. "And you know also how much I love Rufus. I don't want to leave either of you. But most of those men have families too. I *must* think of them! And you *must* listen!"

She bowed her head, her hands still pinned at her sides.

"You are going to die," she answered in a doomed voice which agonized him. "The Romans will kill you and I will never see you again."

He dropped one of her wrists and with his free hand raised her chin till she was forced to look into his eyes once more.

"Don't lose hope. That's wrong! God has—" He stopped, his throat thickening as he remembered that he had not yet described his dream to her. "Leah, a very odd thing happened to me a little while ago when I went to see the Rabbi. I mean, right in the street." And he reported his fainting and God's speaking to him and giving him the mission to free his people from the Roman tyrant.

With a sudden movement she released her wrist from his grip. She said nothing for a few moments, and he thought that perhaps she had not understood.

"The way it happened," he began again, but she shook her head, and he stopped. Yes, she had understood, but there was something else. . . . Did she think he was—

"Leah!" he exclaimed. "I have told you this story exactly the way it happened, but you are silent. You—you don't think I'm mad, do you?"

"No. Did you—does the Rabbi know of this?"

"Yes, I told him immediately, even before admitting that I was the one who attacked the Roman."

"And what did he say?"

"He said that he needed to pray for guidance, and that he would also confer with other rabbis. But in the meantime . . ."

"In the meantime you must give yourself up!" she finished bitterly. "He—he doesn't have much time, does he? I mean to pray and confer. By the time God answers and the rabbis have all made up their minds—"

"God will answer!" he broke in, confidently. "If He spoke to me, He will certainly speak to Rabbi Akiba!"

She turned away from him, deep in thought.

"I still believe the Romans may be bluffing," she said at length. "They may be just trying to frighten us so that one of us" — she faced him again—"like you—will confess and the case will be solved. If that is so, you're acting exactly the way they want you to!"

"I'll wait a few hours," he decided. "Perhaps till tomorrow morning. We still have time. Although Akiba felt I ought to—"

"A plague on Rabbi Akiba!" she screamed again, and his mouth dropped. "Yes, this is how *I* feel," she went on more calmly. "You are not his slave. Why, he himself said you could do just as you wished. Listen to your own conscience and wait till tomorrow! Why, in a few hours there may be another announcement. Perhaps Hadrian in Rome will hear of this and order the release of the hostages. As you have yourself said, he is a learned—"

"I have no real faith in Hadrian," he interrupted roughly. He turned from her and sat down. "Yes, I will wait," he repeated his decision. "Just a few hours may make all the difference." She came near him, put her arm around his shoulder and rested her head on it.

"All the difference," she whispered affectionately. Relief filled her like the breath of life itself.

But next morning the Romans made it clear to the whole city of Jerusalem that they had *not* forgotten the attack on one of them, and that they had every intention of carrying out their threat to the letter. Soon after the sun rose, the hostages, heavily guarded by grim-faced soldiers, were paraded to an open square near the heart of the town. These unfortunate men seemed to take their situation in a variety of ways: some were very brave, while two were on the verge of tears. But all had this in common: a feeling of certainty that this was no mere bluff, but that they would soon die if no one came forward to confess the assault on the Roman. Occasionally one of them darted a frightened glance at the heads of the polished spears of the guards, glinting now in the brightening sunshine. To give up one's life this way, and for something another had done! It was hard to believe this could really happen.

Around them crowded an ever–increasing number of their fellow Jews, pushed back intermittently by the soldiers. Shouts were heard, and curses too, but no one dared as yet to make a single move to rescue them.

Simon, hearing of what was taking place, hurried to the square to observe the scene with his own eyes. He stood there only a little while, for it did not take him long to determine what must be done. Quickly he returned home to say goodbye to Leah and Rufus. He assured her that God would not abandon him, and that in just a little while . . .

As he spoke, there was a knock on the door. Leah

opened it, admitting Akiba and a few other dignitaries whom both she and her husband recognized immediately as the leading rabbis in the land. With them was a young man neither had seen before.

"Thank God I found you here in time!" Akiba exclaimed. "I was afraid that you had already given yourself up."

"I was about to," Simon replied. He put his hand on Lean's shoulder. "This is my wife, Leah."

"You honor us, Rabbi," she said courteously.

"It is a privilege to meet you," he answered. "Do you know Rabbi Gamaliel?" And he introduced them all, including the young man, whose name was Eli. Then he turned in a state of great excitement to Simon. "I have some wonderful news for you! A very remarkable thing happened to me this morning, and I am still having trouble explaining it to myself, let alone the rabbis!"

"What was it?" Simon asked.

"I was studying at home, and suddenly the words grew dark before my eyes. I raised my hand to my head, and for a moment I thought I was going to—faint, like you. Rachel, my wife, was with me in the same room and hurried over to me anxiously. I heard her voice, but quickly that too seemed to fade away, and instead I heard a—a new Voice." He leaned forward and spoke more tensely than ever. "Tell me, Simon, this Voice which you heard yesterday in your dream—did it seem to . . ." He faltered and rubbed his forehead vigorously for a few seconds, as if trying to gather his wits.

Simon, catching his excitement, prompted him: ". . . seem to fill up the whole street, and yet somehow I was sure I alone heard it!"

"Yes!" Akiba replied. "The whole room seemed full

of it, and yet when I looked up at Rachel, I could see she had heard nothing at all.''

"What did it say, Rabbi?''

"It told me to—listen to you. It said you were a true Messiah, and that I must help you in every way I can to throw off forever the tyranny of the Romans!''

Rabbi Gamaliel stirred uncomfortably and mumbled, "A dream! Just a dream." And the elder next to him, Rabbi Bezalel, said more boldly, "Why have we come here?" Akiba wheeled on them both with a fiercer expression than Simon had ever seen on that gentle face, and immediately they were silent. Then he turned back to Simon, continuing:

"My son, I have prayed harder and with more fervor than I have ever prayed for guidance before, and I believe now that this was my answer, that this Voice was that of the Almighty. Simon, listen to me! From this moment on you are to be known throughout Israel as Bar Kochba—Son of a Star."

"Son of a Star?" asked the other, puzzled.

"Don't you know the verse in the Bible? 'A star has come forth from Jacob.' I have always interpreted the line as referring to the Messiah."

A great feeling of humility overwhelmed Simon, and he bowed his head. Leah put her hand on his shoulder.

"But what of the hostages?" she asked Akiba. "If my husband gives himself up to the Romans, they will surely kill him, and what will be the meaning of your Voice then?"

"He is not to give himself up," Akiba answered firmly. "I thank God again I got here in time!" He turned now to Eli, tugged at his sleeve a little and thus brought him forward a step. The young man was a tall, well-built fellow, with quick, intelligent eyes. "This very good friend of ours has offered to take his place, leaving him free to organize a Jewish revolt against Hadrian."

Simon stared at Eli as if seeing him for the very first time.

"You would go in my place?" he asked in astonishment.

Eli smiled.

"Do not look so surprised. I'm really not much of a hero, and don't expect to sacrifice my life for you. According to the plan the rabbis and I have made, as soon as the hostages have been released, your very first duty will be to lead a rescue party to free me as well. If it happens that you should fail—" He shrugged and finished, "I shall have the honor to be among the first of our soldiers to die in the Bar Kochba rebellion." He went on more cheerfully, his voice gathering firmness and strength. "But I do not think you will fail! I am sure that there are many who will follow you, and as for me, I—I happen to believe with Rabbi Akiba that you are a true Messiah. How can one sent by God fail?"

Simon eyed him steadily for a few moments.

"Still," he murmured at length, "whether I am a true Messiah or a false one, you are a very brave man." He reflected another second or two, and then shook his head, frowning.

"What is wrong?" demanded Akiba, frowning also.

"No, this is impossible. I cannot let him risk his life for me this way. Why don't *I* go, as you yourself advised only a few hours ago? Then he can try to rescue *me!*"

"No! That would be nothing more than a rash and needless gamble. Eli has volunteered, and we have accepted his offer with gratitude. He is ready!"

"I certainly am," said Eli. "And I am leaving right now, for time is getting short." He walked to the door.

Simon seized him so strongly he winced with pain.

"You must not! They will kill you!"

Eli removed his grip gently and smiled again.

"Save me then."

He opened the door, stepped out and almost slammed it behind him. Simon made a move to follow him, but Leah pleaded, "Don't!"

"I must save him," he said, facing her.

"You will, my son," Akiba assured him.

Chapter Seven

Eli went to the Romans and, faithful to their pledge, they released the hostages and imprisoned him instead. Simon was about to gather a group of fellow Jews, according to plan, and lead it to rescue him, but another idea came to him. He talked it over with Akiba, who gave him permission to try it. What he wanted to do was approach Tinnius Rufus himself first and plead the cause of his people—in addition, asking him to let Eli go. Several of the other rabbis, hearing of this, scoffed at it, calling it just a waste of time, since the Governor was known to be a very cruel and arrogant man who would listen to no one but Hadrian himself. Besides, there was no telling *when* the Romans would decide to put Eli to death, or punish him in other ways, and each moment was precious.

In the end, however, Simon was allowed to make this one effort to put the case of the Jews before Tinnius. If he failed to persuade him of anything, the very next step was to be the rescue of Eli, and no further schemes could possibly be allowed to delay it any longer.

Getting to see Tinnius was no easy matter, for there were guards all around his headquarters in Jerusalem, and Simon was a stranger to them. But when he told them he came in behalf of Rabbi Akiba, word was sent in to the Governor, and the answer came that he would see him for just a few minutes, if he promised to be brief.

"Very brief," said Simon, and soon he found himself standing erect in front of Tinnius, who sat at a table, busy with some military orders, and at first didn't even seem to see him. He was a large man with heavy jowls and a strong chin. Simon had often seen him before, of course, galloping through the streets at the head of his soldiers, but never so close as this.

At last he looked up.

"You come from Rabbi Akiba?" he asked, almost sleepily.

"Yes, sir."

He leaned back in his chair.

"And what is *your* name, my friend?"

"Simon bar—" He hesitated, remembering the new one which had just been bestowed upon him. "Simon bar Kochba."

The other smiled.

"You had trouble saying that." The sleepiness suddenly vanished from his eyes, and he snapped, "Is Simon bar Kochba your real name?"

"Yes, it is!"

"And why are you here?"

"I want to talk to you about—Eli."

"Eli?" A puzzled expression crossed his face. "And who, may I ask, is Eli?"

"The man you have just imprisoned for attacking the Roman soldier."

Tinnius frowned heavily.

"I see. That was a very foolish thing to do, you know, and he will pay dearly for it." He stared at him. "What have *you* to say about him?"

"I have come to ask you to—release him."

"Release him!" he shouted, dumfounded, and stood up. "Young man, you must be out of your mind." He glanced around as if for a guard.

"Tinnius, you don't understand," Simon said quickly. He studied him again.

"You mean his imprisonment was a—mistake?"

"Yes, a great one! You don't know the whole story. Eli saw this Jewish child being cuffed about by the patrolman, and he tried to stop him, as any man would. But the Roman, without a word, pushed him away. That's why Eli attacked. Now wouldn't you have done the same?"

"No one attacks one of our soldiers, for whatever reason, and goes unpunished!" was the stern reply.

"There is another matter—besides Eli."

"And what is that?"

"This new plan of Hadrian to rebuild Jerusalem—we want you to abandon it."

Tinnius smiled again.

"It is *you* who do not understand. I am just a soldier myself, whom Hadrian commands, and who must obey without daring to question his orders." His eyes dropped to a scroll on his desk. "You will be interested in hearing that there will be more than just this rebuilding in the future. I have here Hadrian's latest edicts." He raised his eyes again to Simon. "From now on, you Jews will not be permitted to study your law nor observe your Sabbath. How does *that* strike you, my friend?"

For a few moments Simon could not even find his

voice. Rage choked him like real hands around his throat.

"We are not permitted to—" he managed at last, but could go no further.

"—study your law nor observe your Sabbath," Tinnius repeated mildly, with a trace of humor.

"But that would take our faith away altogether!" Simon protested. "Is that what—" He stopped again, for the idea which had occurred to him—the thought of what Hadrian might really have in the back of his mind —was such a stunning one it could only be considered calmly. He waited for a few seconds till the rushed beating of his heart slowed down a little and he could speak more normally. "Is that what Hadrian is planning?" he asked, almost as if none of this really concerned him.

The smile on the other's face broadened and he shrugged.

"I'm not going to press him for details." He tapped the scroll meaningfully, his expression becoming serious again. "But let me make something very clear. I *am* going to carry out his orders, and to the letter! My responsibility here as Governor of Judea is very heavy, and he would not have entrusted me with it if he did not consider me entirely worthy of it. I am determined to prove to him he hasn't made a mistake! Well," he finished impatiently, "if that is all you came for . . ."

"Sir, *both* of you are making a mistake!"

Tinnius stared at him.

"Beware, my young friend," he said at length. "I gave you permission to see me because you come from the Rabbi, but I will have none of your impudence. If you go too far . . ."

"What, sir? Will you put me in jail with Eli?"

The Governor's neck began reddening with anger, but Simon went on, for God's message had given him great courage. "Tinnius, in the name of the people of Judea, I demand that Eli be released immediately. I demand also that the rebuilding of Jerusalem be stopped, and that these new edicts you mention be revoked. If these two demands are not met within twenty-four hours, we will—" His voice caught suddenly and he hesitated, for here was a step in a direction from which there could be no turning back.

Tinnius moved quickly from behind his table and faced his visitor squarely. They were of almost exactly the same height, and so they stood eye to eye.

"You will what?" he asked thickly.

But the visitor did not flinch, for he believed with all his heart in the justice of his cause.

"We will revolt," he answered quietly.

Tinnius's head, as if struck by a blow, jerked back, and he took a better look at him.

"Revolt? You?" And suddenly and unexpectedly, he exploded into loud, scornful laughter.

Simon waited patiently till he stopped and then went on fiercely. "Yes, revolt! To us Jews our faith is a very great and serious thing. If you try to take it away, we will risk our lives to defend it! For if you succeed in taking it away, we are no longer Jews, but men without a religion, who in our opinion resemble the beasts of the field. Rather than resemble the beasts of the field, we will fight!"

Tinnius nodded.

"I see. But what if you become like the Romans? We have a faith, too, you know," he said proudly. "We have our gods."

"We prefer our one God to your many."

Tinnius turned around and went back to his table.

"Get out," he murmured. "I am afraid you have already overstayed your welcome."

"You—you will not listen to our plea?"

"I have listened to it long enough. You have nothing further to say."

"Tinnius—"

"Get out!" he roared in exasperation. "Or must I call my guards to assist you? How dare you come here with this silly story of a Jewish revolt? Why, you—you'd be crushed in a few days! What can a handful of ill–equipped Jews hope to accomplish against the might of imperial Rome? Get out! Out!"

Simon knew in that moment that only a show of force would impress this man. Words meant absolutely nothing. A sadness filled him and his face fell, for in an instant he thought of all the fine Jewish young men who must now risk their lives—some of them even give them up—because of the cruel folly of these two tyrants, Hadrian and Tinnius.

He was going to say, "Tinnius, listen to me!" but there was now a look about him which made it perfectly clear that any further entreaty or threats would be completely useless. And so at last he turned and left, his steps sounding loudly in the corridors, as if echoing the heaviness of his heart.

By the time he reached Akiba's home, however, his mood had changed, for there was no time left to be gloomy. Eli was still at the mercy of the Romans and had to be rescued immediately, or he might soon lose his life. Simon reported the failure of his mission to the Rabbi as quickly as possible.

"Tinnius will never understand anything but force!" he finished. "We must now make plans to throw off the Roman yoke forever."

"He—he would not listen you, would he?" Akiba murmured.

"No, Rabbi. He takes his commands from his emperor, and for him even to *think* of disobeying them is out of the question." And he had to tell him also about the new edicts, prohibiting the reading of the Law and the observing of the Sabbath.

Akiba shook his head, as if trying to shake off the shock of this terrible additional blow.

"Then there can be no doubt of the course God wishes us to follow!" he cried, and he sat down and looked up at Simon. "You are young, my son. I can give you my advice, but it is *you* who will have to bear the brunt of the battle. Do you think you will have the—strength, my son, the wisdom?"

"God is with us both!" Simon answered. "He will not fail us, for after all, we are fighting only to hold on to our faith in Him, and pass it on to our children. Yes, I have the strength! I *must* have it. Though we are a small people, our cause is righteous, and there is nothing in this world stronger than a people which believes in what it is fighting for!"

Akiba's eyes lit up with deep pride and happiness.

"I admire your spirit, Simon. I have confidence in you." A thought struck him, and he turned away. "Still, we must face our enemies with more than just a belief in our cause." He eyed him again. "What of weapons? We must have spears, horses—"

Simon smiled.

"Rabbi, you are a great teacher of the Law, but there

are things happening in Judea which you have not heard of. Don't you know that we Jews have been preparing for many years for just such a revolt as this? I am the last to listen to rumors about what the Emperor is planning, but I have always believed in some day driving out every Roman from Judea—and in being *ready* when that day comes."

"Ready? In what way?

"You know, of course, that we have been making arms for the Romans."

"Yes, I know that."

"And many of them are being returned as defective."

"Yes, I've heard of that. In fact, Tinnius himself has complained more than once— Hold on! You mean we have been making them defectively—on purpose?"

Simon nodded.

"You're beginning to get the idea!" he smiled.

"And then you take these weapons and—correct them so that they can be used—by us?"

"Yes."

"Do you have many of them by now?"

This time Simon grinned broadly.

"Thousands! We have a few secret collections all over Jerusalem. Would you like to see one of them? It is not far from here."

Akiba stood up.

"Yes, I would. I—" He stopped. "No, Simon," he went on, his tone changing. "In these matters I shall trust you. But what of the new army itself? Can you assemble it?"

"There are many who will join with me immediately, and others will soon follow, as soon as they hear of the new edicts. But first of all what I shall need is a small band of loyal followers who will help me rescue Eli."

"Gather it, then, Simon, and God be with you!"

Simon turned and hurried to the door. There he paused and faced Akiba again.

"This will be our first blow for freedom," he said, "and none too soon. It is time we rid ourselves of these foreign masters!"

Akiba joined him at the door.

"We will win," he predicted confidently. "God, Who has spoken so clearly to both of us, will never abandon us in these days of terrible struggle!"

Chapter Eight

Simon moved fast. He made a list of twelve very able and wide-awake men whom he knew he could rely on in the effort to rescue Eli, and he called on them one by one. Only two of them seemed hesitant, but just in the beginning. Soon Simon was able to persuade even these of the great importance of the job which faced them, and they joined forces with the rest.

If they were to be successful, night was the best time for it, Simon was certain, for the darkness would be their friend: the guards who would stand in their way would be a little less alert, a little sleepier. Even the Romans were human!

And so that very evening, armed with weapons carefully chosen from one of the secret collections he had just described to the Rabbi, he led this brave band of patriots to the prison near the outskirts of Jerusalem where Eli was being held. Guards surrounded the place, to be sure, but Simon noticed with a thrill of happiness that they were fewer than he had expected. Stealthily he led his men toward the gate, for this was the only entrance by which they could hope to get in. At the moment there were only two Romans in front of it, the rest circling the prison. Simon signaled his troops to keep their heads low and out of sight, tossed a stone against the side of the somber-looking building and then hid himself too.

Glancing up, he saw no reaction in the behavior of the guards. He threw another stone, and this time they looked curiously at the side of the building, turned to each other and whispered for a few moments. Then one of them, to investigate, moved closer to the spot where the stone had struck. Another signal from Simon to his comrades, and they leaped up and followed him to the gate as fast as they could. The lone guard remaining, spotting them, called frantically to his fellow soldier, but before he could even finish the shout, a hand was over his mouth and he was sprawling in the dust under one of the attacking band. Another stood over him threateningly with a spear, and a third quickly relieved him of his keys. In another moment the gate was open and ten men, led by Simon, raced into the prison. The other two dragged the sentry behind the gate, closed it and watched him, lest he try to sound the alarm again. But the Roman seemed now to prefer caution, especially with the point of a spear at his throat, and he simply lay there, glaring up at his captors, in hostile silence. Even when the hand was removed from his mouth, he chose to stay quiet.

The invaders dashed through the prison, peering into one cell after another until they heard Eli cry, "Simon! This way!" Simon thanked God he was still alive and followed the voice to his cell. The right key was found at last, the door was swung open and Eli stepped out, taking a deep breath of relief.

"I knew you would be here!" he told Simon gratefully. "Do you see? I wasn't wrong when I offered to take your place."

"We're not out of here yet," the other replied grimly. "This is only halfway. Come on!"

They sped back to the gate. As they approached it, they heard a clamor and feared the worst. The sentry who had gone to investigate the stone had returned to the gate and, finding his ally missing, sounded the alarm. In a few moments, Simon and his band realized, all of those guards would be at the gate. But as if God were indeed watching the Jews, the moon suddenly disappeared behind a thick black cloud, leaving everything under a black, protective mantle.

"Now is the time to get out!" Simon whispered, and he lunged through the gate, the rest hard on his heels. They were not a second too soon, for the Romans came running up, their spears poised. But they could not see the Jews, and only heard steps scuttling off in the darkness. They followed the sound of them through the streets of the city until even that faded in the distance. Then, shamefaced to the point of not even being able to look at each other, they had to give up the chase and return to their posts empty-handed and dreading the moment Tinnius received the report of the rescue.

That night the word spread among the people of Jerusalem that Eli had been saved, and that Simon was now recruiting a strong force of Jewish soldiers to begin an open rebellion against the Romans. Young men by the hundreds sought him out and some even begged for the privilege of joining him. With Eli at his side, he worked feverishly till early in the morning, planning to strike again before Tinnius had a chance to recover from his surprise and cast about for a way of hitting back.

By dawn over a thousand recruits were with him, and each hour brought many more. It seemed there was hardly a youth in all of Jerusalem who did not long to share in the fierce contest ahead of them. Even youngsters hardly big enough to carry a spear flocked to him, but these, of course, were turned away, as were men too old to ride and soldier.

At noon Simon and Eli headed a picked group against a street patrol of Romans and drove them back to their barracks, felling many on the way. Tinnius instantly sounded the alarm, and the war was on in earnest. In an hour the city resounded with the sound of spear striking spear, the neighing of horses and the cries of the wounded and dying. Simon moved in again and again where the fighting was thickest, using his great strength to strike down one Roman after another. Inspired by his example, his troops fought more courageously than ever. By nightfall most of the city was in Jewish hands. Tinnius had fled from his quarters, and now occupied a house very near the border of the city.

His fury at what had suddenly happened to him was equalled only by his shame and humiliation. Who could have imagined that this upstart people, this mere handful of impudent Jews—

He called in one of his centurions, Cornelius.

"How do you explain it?" he demanded.

Cornelius, a tall young man who had served for years in the Roman army as faithfully as he could, found himself, however, no match for such a question.

"I—I don't know," he fumbled, wishing he were a far wiser soldier.

"But you must have some ideas," the other insisted.

"We've just spent the day fighting with them. Can't you think of a single thing—didn't you notice a clue—"

Luckily for Cornelius—Tinnius was not noted for patience—a thought came to him.

"Those spears!" he exclaimed.

"What about them?"

"They're ours, aren't they? They're made just like the ones we have."

The Governor frowned, still puzzled.

"What are you driving at?"

"You know the Jews have been making our spears for a long time. What was to prevent them—"

"Stop! I see where you're headed. They've been sending us only a fraction of what they've been making and keeping the rest for themselves!"

"There's more to it than that. Remember how many of them we've had to send back because they just weren't good enough? What was to keep the Jews from taking these and *making* them good enough?"

Tinnius sat down, considering this.

"If this is what they've been doing . . ." he thought aloud. "Why," he went on, turning back to Cornelius, "they could have made thousands this way!"

"Thousands," the centurion nodded.

Tinnius continued to ponder the matter, and then said, "Still, weapons alone can't account for the way they're fighting. They seem to have a—a kind of spirit in them that makes each one fight with the fury of ten. How do you explain that?"

"I heard you met their leader, Bar Kochba."

"Yes, he came to see me just the other day."

"Was he the sort to give men that spirit?"

"He seemed like a man with a mission," Tinnius nodded.

"Perhaps that too, then, explains the success of the Jews. If they have excellent leadership—"

"We must capture Bar Kochba at all costs!" Tinnius interrupted fiercely. "Once he is our prisoner, Jerusalem will soon be ours again."

"I have also heard that the Jews consider him a Messiah."

"A Messiah?"

"Yes. According to their faith, if they are unhappy and oppressed, a great man, a Messiah, will one day come to save them from their oppressors."

"And what of Akiba? When Bar Kochba visited me, he said he spoke for Rabbi Akiba."

"He should be captured too. I am sure he acts as an adviser to Bar Kochba, and together they stir up the people to revolt."

Tinnius, becoming angrier and angrier, got up again and began striding back and forth.

"Revolt! Who would have dreamed they would have the courage? And now we're actually on the run—we, the Romans!" He clenched his fist. "But not for long, Cornelius! Tomorrow will be ours. If each of them fights like ten, each of us must fight like twenty—forty. No wretched rabble is going to make me look like a bumbling fool in the eyes of Hadrian!" He stopped, thinking of how the Emperor would receive the news of this unexpected rebellion. Why, there was no telling *what* he might decide to do. He might even send a new Governor to take his place!

At this moment Simon, of course, was in a very different mood from Tinnius's. He had made his new headquarters in a building abandoned just an hour ago by the

Romans, and the taste of the day's triumphs was still very sweet in his mouth. More than that, he looked forward eagerly to his next thrust at the enemy—a move which, if successful, would push it out of the city altogether.

Just a few hours of vigorous fighting side by side had made Eli and him as close a couple of friends as if they had known each other for years. Simon knew he could trust Eli with his life, and the other, especially after his rescue, had the same feeling about Simon. Flushed with their victorious advance, they could not help discussing it, at the same time trying not to let pride make them too sure of themselves. After all, the war was far from over. They sat at a table sipping wine.

"Our new soldiers!" said Simon, an exultant catch in his tone. "Did you ever see such courage?"

"They were wonderful," Eli agreed. "We could not have asi_d any more of them."

"They're resting now, and well they deserve to . . . Would it be wise at this point to tell them how pleased we are with them?"

Eli reflected.

"Maybe we ought to—wait."

"You mean if we congratulate them too soon and too warmly, they won't do so well the next time?"

"There's something in that, isn't there?"

"I'm sure they know themselves how well they're doing, and we don't really have to tell them. Just imagine! If they go on as they have been . . ."

"They will! Today's victory proves to them that the Romans can be defeated, and from now on there'll be no stopping them." He shook his head. "Hadrian made a very foolish move when he issued those decrees, and he will live to regret them. Why, he must think our faith is a plaything, such as one takes away from children!" He smiled. "Soon he will learn that we are not mere children but grown men ready to risk our lives to protect the religion we were raised in."

"Do you think Tinnius has already told him of our attack?"

"I doubt it. He's probably too ashamed."

"Still, if we continue to push him out of Jerusalem—yes, even out of Judea . . ."

"Word must reach Hadrian sooner or later."

"When that happens, he will probably send reinforcements."

"By that time we ourselves will be much stronger—fresh recruits are joining us every hour—and we will be able to hurl back the reinforcements also!"

Simon had to smile too.

"I see you have every confidence in what we are doing."

"I believe," said Eli seriously, "we are fighting for a very just cause, and that God is with us every moment of the day and night. He will not abandon those who shed their blood for the freedom to worship Him in peace. Besides . . ."

"What?" Simon encouraged him.

"I agree with Rabbi Akiba that you are our Messiah, and that you have been sent by God to deliver us, as you have just delivered me from the Roman dungeon." As his friend was silent, he added, "And you, Simon—you still believe God has entrusted you with this mission to free us, don't you?"

"Yes, Eli. I do!" he answered strongly.

"Have you . . ." He hesitated again, searching for words, for these were awesome matters, and he did not want to say something which failed to express his exact meaning.

"Have I what?" Simon urged him once more.

"Have you heard the Voice of God since that—first time on your way to Akiba?"

"No, Eli, I haven't," Simon was compelled to admit.

"But you still feel . . ."

"I still feel He is very much with me, guiding every step I take."

"But if it happens that we have a—setback or two, will you—still feel the same?"

"Of course!" he exclaimed instantly. "God is no pagan idol to be forgotten the moment things don't go just the way we want them."

Eli stood up and stretched himself with a sudden sense of brimming happiness.

"Simon, what a city this will be when the Romans have been driven completely out of it!" he cried, his eyes shining. "We'll be able to walk the streets again, just as in the old days, with no enemy patrols watching every move we make, telling us what to do, keeping us from our Sabbath!"

"Yes," the other agreed. "It's a wonderful dream, and well worth fighting for. . . . But now, my friend, let's get some sleep, or tomorrow we won't be good for any fighting at all!"

Chapter Nine

Just a few hours later, shortly before dawn, Simon awoke, stirred Eli awake too and ordered him to alert their forces for a new attack. In a matter of minutes they were ready. Simon gave the signal, and they stole toward the enemy. The sentries, some of whom nodded sleepily over their spears, came to life with a start, shouted "Jews! Jews!" and the battle stirred and flamed again, as if there had been no lull at all. Once more the harassed Romans were on the defensive, paying heavily each inch of the way. Their officers cursed and goaded them as fiercely as they could, but to no avail. Slowly they found themselves being thrust back by a strength they never dreamed the Jews possessed. By the time this new attack was over, Tinnius had been pushed to a point a mile outside of Jerusalem, though there were still occasional bursts of scattered fighting within its borders. He wanted to rage and scream at his centurions, but instead managed to control himself and sat quietly trying to get used to the idea of having been driven from this subject city he had ruled for so many years. Nor was this to be the end! Bar Kochba had made it very clear during his visit—had he not?—that he wanted him and his men out of the country altogether!

Several officers, led by Cornelius, approached him, for they had been discussing their shameful retreat and had a suggestion.

"Tinnius," began Cornelius.

The Governor looked up, his eyes a little filmy and distant, for he was still rather shocked by what had happened.

"Yes?"

"We agree that we should send a messenger at once."

"A messenger?"

"Yes, at once—to Hadrian. He should know what is happening. As soon as he—"

"No!" Tinnius interrupted with a roar. "Hadrian has other matters to worry him. We will rest here a few hours and then hammer our way back into the city!"

Another centurion, a short, dark-faced man, stepped forward.

"But Tinnius, we—we don't feel we can take back Jerusalem from Bar Kochba without—reinforcements."

"Reinforcements!" he exclaimed scornfully. "I am not yet ready for those. No, Lucius, you are asking for—" A thought stopped him, and he eyed him closely, and then turned the same look slowly on the others. "Can it be, great officers of the Roman army, that you are—*afraid?*"

Cornelius, stung, straightened.

"It isn't fear that makes us want to send word to Hadrian," he answered quickly. "We are all good soldiers, but we know our strength. We believe it is foolish to gamble needlessly with the troops we have, when we can use them to much better advantage once we are joined by fresh forces dispatched by Hadrian."

"I see. And what makes you think he has fresh forces to send?"

A third centurion, who had not yet spoken, now stepped forward too and almost pleaded, "Publius Marcellus, Legate of Syria, would be of great help to us. If you could ask the Emperor to order him here at the head of a picked division—"

"Ah!" Tinnius interrupted again. "Now I have it—this plan you have been discussing so wisely among yourselves. Why, you have even decided on the very man to come galloping to our rescue!"

The others looked at each other for a few moments, as if wondering what their next move ought to be, for it was clear that their commander was simply too ashamed to beg Hadrian to save him from further defeats at the hands of a subject people he was supposed to be governing. Still, these defeats *were* taking place, Roman blood *was* being spilled, and something had to be done. Nor was there much time to be spent in hesitation and argument. At last, tightening his mouth and using as firm a tone as he dared, Cornelius replied, "Yes, sir, we are all agreed on this. We are sure that if things continue as they are, there won't be a Roman left in Judea within just a few weeks—perhaps days!"

Tinnius sprang angrily to his feet, for the other's tone, as well as words, had cut very deeply.

"Cornelius," he shouted, "you forget yourself! Remember who you are! I am still the Governor of Judea, and if I decide that . . ." His voice suddenly became husky and faltered as he noticed the unfriendly stares of the centurions, though Cornelius lowered his eyes as if half-sorry about his frankness. Tinnius turned away, exploring the situation as thoroughly as he could and trying not to neglect any side of it which might offer a way out. As a governor, he knew quite well he could not really afford to make enemies out of his own officers. These were the men he had to rely on in the thick of fighting as well as in the calm of a quiet meeting, and it would be worse to lose their loyalty than a thousand men in battle.

He faced them again.

"Publius Marcellus, you say," he murmured, considering the suggestion.

Encouraged, Cornelius raised his eyes to him again and blurted, "Yes! With him on our side, Bar Kochba wouldn't have a chance! You'd be back in your palace in Jerusalem in a week!"

Tinnius smiled.

"All right," he agreed suddenly, nodding. "We'll send a messenger to Hadrian—immediately."

The centurions looked at each other again and this time they broke into smiles too. Now, they were sure, Bar Kochba's fate was sealed and the captured city would be theirs again. In a few minutes a messenger, Lucius, had been chosen and was galloping toward Rome.

Hadrian received the news of the rebellion with surprise and anger. He agreed that Publius Marcellus would be a good choice for the one to help bring the Jews under his heel again, and sent Lucius on to Syria with this order. Publius himself, however, did not exactly welcome it. A tall man, bearded and distinguished-looking, he had just finished reviewing his troops in an open field when Lucius appeared with the message from Hadrian. After reading it carefully, he asked Lucius, "What is the matter with Tinnius anyway? I've always given him credit for a great deal of military sense. Why can't he take back his city with*out* my help?"

"You don't know the Jewish soldiers these days," the officer replied. "They're fighting like lions!"

"Lions," the other repeated. "What's got into them anyway? Word of the revolt has reached me, but I never really understood the reason for it. You've been with Tinnius for some time, haven't you?"

"Yes, sir—for years."

"Can you explain it then?"

"The revolt?"

"Yes."

"There is a religious side to it."

"Religious! Oh, I remember now. It's those edicts of Hadrian's. The Jews haven't exactly taken to them, have they?"

"No, Publius, they haven't."

"But to risk their lives for just a couple of orders . . ."

"If you will permit me to say so, sir, to the Jews the edicts are much more than 'just a couple of orders.' If carried out to the letter, they would stop their religious observances and therefore in the end destroy their religion altogether."

Publius eyed him closely.

"You told me your name a minute ago. Lucius, wasn't it?"

"Yes, sir."

"How do *you* feel about the—edicts?"

"I, sir?"

"Yes, Lucius," he said sharply. *"You."*

The centurion hesitated.

"I—I do not consider them wise. But then," he added hastily, "who am I to judge these matters? If Hadrian wishes to deprive the Jews of their faith, that is his affair, and we soldiers can only do our duty and obey. Perhaps he has plans we are not able to understand yet. It is our job as good officers to trust him in everything he does."

"But if these orders had not been issued, there would be no Jewish revolt now and I could stay on here in Syria."

"That is true, Publius," Lucius nodded. "But one must face things as they come."

Regretfully Publius looked about the field, ringed by the beautiful, pine-forested slopes in the distance.

"I shall be sorry to leave," he murmured at length. "I have been happy here."

"I can understand that."

Lucius waited a few moments, and then stirred impatiently. "Hadrian wishes that you gather some of your best troops—"

The other silenced him with a look.

"I have read the message. Are you going back to him now?"

"As soon as I have your answer."

"Tell him I am moving immediately to Judea to—" He smiled with a trace of bitterness. "To rescue Tinnius."

Lucius hesitated again.

"Shall I use the word—'rescue?' "

Publius thought about the word, his face hardening gradually.

"Yes, use it! I still believe Tinnius should have done a much better job of governing the Jews, edicts or no edicts!"

Within an hour he headed a strong division of his troops in full gallop toward Judea. As he rode, his mind returned again and again to the difficult job which faced him, and he could not help continuing to feel bitter about being pulled out of a fairly comfortable situation, where he was very much in command and having no real trouble, to a place where even the wisest general could not really predict the outcome. Suppose, like Tinnius—dreadful thought!—he were defeated by Bar Kochba too, driven back from stronghold to stronghold! The whole empire would rock with the news, which might even touch off new revolts among subject peoples who up to now had been too frightened to raise a finger.

The more he thought about what lay ahead for him, the less he liked it. And the less he liked it, the angrier he was with Tinnius who, in his opinion, was largely responsible for his present plight. Therefore, by the time he approached his camp near Jerusalem, he was in a very evil mood indeed.

At the sound of hoof beats, a guard near Tinnius's tent spread the word and everybody sprang to the alert, for these might be Jews attacking from the rear. But when Publius's soldiers, in Roman uniforms, appeared, Tinnius breathed a sigh of relief, for he felt that now, with the help of these reinforcements, it would not be long before the city was back in the palm of his hand, where it belonged. He stepped forward with a smile to greet the Legate and received a cordial enough greeting in return. In a minute the two soldiers were sitting at a table in the tent, alone and sipping wine. Publius kept on his mask of friendliness, but soon enough he lowered it slowly.

"Tell me your side of the story, Tinnius," he urged. "There you were, the Jews trembling every time you rode by in the street, and now you are camped out here like a—a refugee. How do you explain it?"

Tinnius took another sip of wine.

"Haven't you heard? Hadrian's edicts—"

"Yes, I know all about the edicts!" the other broke in sharply. "But you're supposed to be a Governor, aren't you? Why couldn't you enforce them?"

Tinnius reddened at the unexpected onslaught. For a moment he was tempted to hurl back an equally sharp answer, but he restrained himself and smiled.

"You don't understand the situation here, Publius. We are dealing with a very strange and remarkable people."

"What's so strange about them? I've been here before, and they seemed as peaceable a nation as you can find anywhere."

Tinnius reddened again, and this time he could not hold back his anger.

"Peaceable!" he flashed. "You should have been here yesterday, and you would have seen with your own eyes how peaceable they are when they think they have something worth fighting for!"

"What *are* they fighting for?" As Tinnius opened his mouth to reply, Publius waved him into silence. "Oh, yes, their religion. Your messenger, Lucius, told me something about that. Still, you *are* the Governor, and if they were really afraid of you, no one would have dared *dream* of a revolt, let alone start one."

"Well, they've dreamed and they've started," Tinnius smoldered. "I doubt that if you had been in my place you would have done better."

"I *would* have done better!" Publius almost snarled, pushing his cup away with a violent movement. "I know people and I know how to handle them."

"You don't know *these* people," Tinnius insisted. "They have some excellent leaders."

"Yes, I've heard of them—especially the one called

Son of a Star—Bar Kochba." He spoke more mildly: "What's he like? Have you met him?"

"He's a fanatic. He thinks he can actually . . ." He stopped.

Publius smiled.

"Actually what? Chase you out of Jerusalem?"

The Governor leaned forward a little, choosing his words carefully. "It isn't just that he seems to know a lot about—fighting. He—he has a great faith in himself, and the other Jews feel it and follow him, for they believe in him as much as he believes in himself. Why, he even has the rabbis believing in him—especially Rabbi . . ."

"Rabbi who?" Publius rasped. "Don't you remember? It will be important when we capture them all."

"Akiba. That's it—Rabbi Akiba."

"How much do you know about him?"

"Akiba?"

"Yes."

"Not very much. Except that . . ."

"Go on," Publius urged.

"I have heard that Bar Kochba thinks he himself is a kind of—Messiah, and that Akiba believes he is too. Together they've persuaded—"

"Messiah? What's that?"

"It means 'Anointed One.' The Jews believe that a great deliverer, a Messiah, will some day come and rescue them from their oppressors."

"You mean they feel *we* are their oppressors these days, and that Bar Kochba will deliver them from *us?*"

Tinnius nodded.

"Exactly! And when a faith like that spreads among hundreds of thousands of people—why, it's like a madness, and there's no holding them!"

Publius folded his hands and rubbed his bearded chin thoughtfully with his thumb.

"I see . . . They *are* different," he had to admit at length.

Tinnius smiled in relief, beginning to feel again as he had when they first greeted each other.

"You do see, don't you? That is why we had to call on Hadrian for reinforcements. Wouldn't you have done the same?"

Yet the Legate stiffened and replied sternly, still not convinced, "Let us plan our next attack together now. As soon as I've met the Jews on the battlefield and seen for myself how they fight, I shall be able to judge better what sort of general you have been up to now."

"Good enough!" Tinnius exclaimed heartily, and refilled his cup of wine for him. Publius looked at it for a moment, raised it and sipped it slowly and reflectively.

Chapter Ten

In spite of their plans, however, it was Simon again who attacked next, sending them staggering from one village to another and giving them the sinking feeling that no matter how many more troops Hadrian tried to spare from other countries, this young upstart would always win. Tinnius and Publius sat and consulted and conferred, but to no avail. Each time the actual fighting began it was they who were on the defensive and Simon who did the pushing. Was there no holding him? Would they have to eat crow together and beg Hadrian for more help?

One evening, as Simon sat in his tent plotting his next move, he had an unexpected visitor. He was already quite a distance from Jerusalem, and the last person on earth he expected to see in the middle of a battlefield was his wife Leah. And yet Leah it was!

His guards noticed her first and, not recognizing her, challenged her.

"Who's there?" one called.

"It is I, Leah—wife of Bar Kochba."

She took a few steps forward toward them and then stopped, while the soldiers inspected her.

"Wait here," one said. He turned and brought news of her arrival to Simon, who came out immediately, at first so surprised and happy to see her that he forgot to scold her for taking such foolish and unnecessary risks.

"Leah!" he almost shouted. "What are you doing here?" But before she could answer, he had his arm around her and was leading her back into his tent. Inside, he turned to her again and looked her up and down. "How wonderful to see you again!" he smiled and then, in almost the next instant, frowned. "What madness took hold of you to make you come here in the midst of all this fighting? Why, there are enemy patrols all around!"

"Simon, I *had* to come."

"Why? What's wrong?" A thought struck him. "Is it—something about Rufus? Tell me," he went on anxiously. "Is he all right?"

She smiled reassuringly.

"He's fine. And he is the envy of all his classmates for having such a hero for a father!"

"Hero," he repeated, shaking his head. "I only do God's will."

"Simon, what about you? How do *you* feel?"

"I? Splendid! Things have been going so well for us I'd be a fool to complain about *any*thing. And yet . . ." He stopped.

"What is it, Simon?" she urged.

"Sometimes I have my doubts as to—to what we are doing."

"Doubts?"

"Yes. When one of us dies, I—I can't help feeling—responsible."

"You mean because you started the revolt."

He nodded.

"Yes."

"But—God told you to start it, didn't He?"

He said nothing for a few moments, and then admitted, "Leah, I—I need Rabbi Akiba. Have you—seen him lately?"

"No, I haven't, except from a distance. Why do you need him, Simon?"

"He must tell me I am right, that our cause is a just one, that God is still with us."

She put her hand on his arm.

"God—hasn't spoken to you since that first time, has He?"

"No, Leah, He hasn't. I thought at first that this would make no difference, and that even if I never heard His Voice again, I would always feel His Presence with us. Lately, though . . ."

"You have had your doubts."

"Yes. But here I am, talking about myself, and still not knowing what made you risk your life to come here!"

"Only that I had to see you. It seems like months since we last laid eyes on each other, and yet the calendar says it's only weeks. How much you have accomplished in so short a time! Why, Simon, you are the most famous man in Jerusalem!"

He smiled.

"My purpose here is not to become famous, but to free our people of the Romans."

"I know. And you will! I *know* you will!"

He sat down, inviting her to do the same.

"You must be hungry," he said as she did.

"First I must learn more about your need for Akiba.

Why don't you go back to Jerusalem for a few days? Then you could—"

"No, no, that's impossible!" he interrupted, shaking his head. "I must keep attacking the Romans while we have the advantage; otherwise they will have a chance to recover, and then our job will be doubly difficult— triply."

"I'll tell him you want to talk to him again!" she exclaimed.

He looked at her.

"You?"

"Of course! What could be a better plan? I'm going back anyway, and as soon as I'm there, I'll visit him and tell him how you feel. I am sure he will send back word—"

"No," he broke in once more. "Since I know the sort of man he is, there's no question in my mind that he will try to come here himself. And I don't have to tell you again how dangerous that is!"

"Still, if you send soldiers to accompany him . . ."

He reflected.

"That would certainly be the only way," he agreed. "The same soldiers who escort you back to Jerusalem could escort the Rabbi here. Very well," he decided. "Visit him . . . And now—let us eat!" he grinned. "Let's enjoy these few precious minutes together, while we still have them." He called for one of the guards to bring them some wine and roast lamb, and soon they were savoring and chuckling over a deliciously tasty meal almost as if they were back home in Jerusalem—except, of course, that Rufus was not there to enjoy it with them.

When the time came for goodbyes, however, their spirits sagged. He warned her almost fiercely not to try to make her way to the front lines again, as his forces were pushing farther and farther from the city, thus steadily increasing the danger of such journeys. She promised to obey and set out once again for Jerusalem, surrounded by four stalwart soldiers and riding with a fifth. It turned out to be a rough and hazardous trip, for more than once they had to stop when they heard suspicious noises which sounded like Romans, and wait cautiously till it seemed safe to move again.

At last she was home, grateful to be back, and embraced Rufus. She told him all about the visit, except for the part about Simon's doubts. Next morning she called at Akiba's home. Rachel, his wife, let her in.

"I am Leah, wife of Simon Bar Kochba," she introduced herself.

"Simon's wife!" Rachel exclaimed warmly. "Of course, I think I've seen you a few times, but we've never really talked, have we? Please sit down."

"Thank you." She did so, and went on, "I came to see the Rabbi."

"He's in the next room. Have you heard from your husband lately?"

Leah smiled.

"I met him yesterday."

"Met him!" Her eyes widened with astonishment. "But how could you? You mean he—came back?"

"No, he didn't. But *I* went to see *him!*"

At this moment the Rabbi, hearing voices, opened the door. Leah stood up.

"This is Leah, wife of Bar Kochba," Rachel told him. And she turned back to her, staring. "She says she just saw—her husband."

The Rabbi smiled cordially.

"How are you, Leah?"

"I am well, but Simon needs you."

"Let me understand this. You went to the front to visit him?"

"Yes, Rabbi. And he sent me back with an escort of five soldiers to make sure I arrived safe. I bear a message from him."

He glanced at her hands.

"Where is it?"

"It is a word of mouth one. Rabbi, he needs you! He —he doubts himself sometimes; thinks God is not with him any more."

"But he is doing so well in battle! How can he question —" He stopped. "Or do you bring news that he is losing ground?"

"No, the news is still wonderful!" she laughed. "The Romans are in full retreat, abandoning one village after another like frightened mice."

"Good." He frowned. "Then why does he doubt himself? I don't understand."

"It is true we are routing the enemy, but not without paying a high price. Some of our men, many of them among Simon's oldest and closest friends, have already given their lives. And each time one of them falls—"

Akiba raised his hand.

"I see. He—he blames himself."

"Yes, Rabbi."

"It shows he has a great heart. And yet we all knew when we began the revolt that we could not hope to win without some heavy sacrifices."

"But when they actually happen, they are very hard to bear."

"True." He sat down, stroking his beard thoughtfully.

"I wish I could be of help to him!" he murmured. "I want so much to be of help."

"You can be. Go to him!" she urged. "The soldiers who brought me here would be glad to escort you directly to his side."

"He needs my prayers," he went on. "If I could only see him, even if only for a little while—"

"How can you see him?" Rachel exclaimed excitedly. "Wouldn't it be enough to send him a few messages? The journey would be too much for you! Think of the danger!"

"Please, Rachel," he answered, "do not be alarmed." His eyes twinkled. "I am already eighty years old, and if God had wished to take me, He would have done so a long time ago. Besides, those soldiers of ours will guard me as if I were their own father—or perhaps grandfather —for they know it is for Simon's sake." He turned to Leah. "Won't they?"

"You can trust them with your life!" she assured him.

"Where are they now?"

"They will be at my home in an hour. If you can be ready by then—"

"An hour!" cried Rachel.

He stood up and put his arm around her, comforting her.

"Please, my dear wife. Where is your faith in God? Don't you believe He will watch over me and see that I return safe to you?"

She buried her face teafully in his shoulder, too upset to reply. He patted her arm gently. "You'll see, Rachel," he promised. "I'll be back before you even *begin* to miss me!"

Chapter Eleven

He met the soldiers at Leah's home and soon they were on their way. Not being an experienced horseman, he rode with one of the soldiers, and every once in a while they slowed up a little to permit him to rest. The man he rode with, Joshua, praised Simon as if he were almost a god rather than just a human being, and gave Akiba the feeling that Simon's doubts about himself were shared with none of his men, but remained as hidden as a very personal secret. This, the Rabbi thought, was as it should be, for there was no point in worrying a fighting army with more troubles than it already had.

They were about halfway to Simon's quarters when the sound of hoof beats in the distance stopped them. Taking cover instantly behind some trees, they waited to see whether it was Romans or Jews. Luckily it was a Jewish patrol, and they hailed and soon joined it.

At last they arrived at Simon's tent. Simon came out and greeted Akiba warmly.

"Rabbi! You decided to come."

"Yes, I did, my son. Leah gave me your message, and

I got here as soon as I could." He nodded toward Joshua. "You have quite an admirer here."

"Joshua?" Simon smiled. "A very loyal man. Did you have any trouble on the way? But let us discuss this in my tent." They went in and Simon asked, "Would you like some wine? You look a little tired."

"If you please, my son. I *am* a bit thirsty."

In a minute they sat sipping their wine and enjoying each other's company almost as if there were no war at all. Simon was glad to hear that the other's journey had not been disturbed by any unusual incidents. "We've just about cleared out the Romans between here and Jerusalem," he announced proudly, "but there's always the chance of a few stragglers, and it is not wise to forget this."

"Your men took excellent care of me. I have no complaints at all."

"Fine!"

Simon glanced at the other's cup.

"Would you like some lamb as well?"

"In a little while, perhaps, Simon. Right now I'd just like to drink my wine and—talk." He said nothing for a few moments, wondering how he could best bring up the object of his visit. At last he went on, "These doubts you speak of, Simon—doubts about yourself, your mission . . ."

"Yes, Rabbi."

"How long have you had them?"

"Only in the last week or so."

"Has anything—special happened to bring them on?"

"No, I don't think so, Rabbi. It's just a general feeling that I get that maybe I—I'm not really the man for this job."

"Leah tells me that several of your closest friends have already fallen. This—must have shocked you."

"Of course."

"To the point you felt that perhaps you were not really the—Messiah?"

Simon set down his cup, looking as deeply into himself as he could.

"Yes, Rabbi," he admitted.

"But if God's Voice told you plainly you were, how can you doubt His word now?"

"In the midst of all this fighting, one can doubt anything, even that God spoke to me."

"But you are driving back the enemy! You are succeeding beyond your brightest dreams! Doesn't that prove to you that you are doing His work?

"Most of the time it does, but there are these moments . . . Rabbi, I asked you to make your dangerous trip here so that you could stand beside me and help me. You—yourself still believe I am the Messiah, don't you?"

"More than ever!"

"But Rabbi, how can you be so—sure?"

"You forget, Simon. I too have heard the Voice, telling me that you are a true Messiah, and that I must help you throw off forever the tyranny of the Romans."

"Yes, I remember now! You told me that the day you came over with Eli to save the hostages."

"And if God speaks to us both, how can we forget His Voice? Are we two children that He has to speak to us each day to remind us of our duty?"

Simon bowed his head.

"I am sorry, Rabbi."

Akiba reached over and patted his shoulder.

"You need not be," he assured him. "Even the best of

us question ourselves when great sacrifices must be made." He stood up. "A little while ago, I thought all had to do was visit you and then go back immediately to Jerusalem. But I see now that you need me by your side until the war is won. Simon, I will pray for you again and again until all your doubts are settled, and you know in your heart that what you are doing must be done for the safety and happiness of our people!" He looked about the tent. "Is there a place for an old man here?"

Simon seized his hands and pressed them gratefully.

"You will stay with me—give me your courage, your inspiration every day! Why, you will be worth more than a whole army to me!"

Akiba smiled.

"Do not overestimate my help, my son. It is God who is really helping you, not I."

"But I need you to speak to Him for me!" He stood up too, jubilant, and raised a powerful, menacing fist. "Tinnius and Publius may think they have had a hard time up to now, but that's nothing compared to what's in store for them. Rabbi, I feel ten times stronger already!" Akiba laughed outright, sharing Simon's exultation, but then suddenly a thought came to him and his face clouded. "What's the matter?"

"I—I have been forgetting my wife Rachel. I promised her I'd be back as soon as I could. But now, if I am to stay with you . . ."

"We'll send word, explaining how necessary you are to me! From what I have heard of her, she is a brave, fine woman, and I am sure she will understand."

"Yes," Akiba agreed, "her mind will understand, but her heart—will find it very difficult to accept this." His expression hardened. "Still, if our country is to be rescued, I must do all I can, or I would not consider myself a true rabbi in Israel. Simon, let's send word to her right away!"

Simon excused himself for a moment as he stepped out to find a guard and give him the order, while the Rabbi sat down to consider his new situation, knowing he must do his duty and yet realizing also it would probably be quite some time before he would see his beloved Rachel again.

During the next few days there was a noticeable change in Simon. With Akiba at his side, he no longer felt these burning doubts which made him hesitate each time he had to issue a command. As a result, his army, which had grown steadily with constant reinforcements from all over Judea until it numbered half a million men, fought even more valiantly than ever. Though up to the Rabbi's arrival it had been astonishingly successful, now it pushed away at the Romans with an overwhelming strength which convinced Simon that God was indeed on their side, and that the completely Jewish occupation and rule of the country was only a matter of time. Village after village, fortress after fortress crumbled and fell under the bludgeoning blows of Simon's men, and gradually the land was cleared of the enemy.

News of these victories was rushed back to Jerusalem, and there was no limit to the rejoicing there. Even Leah and Rachel, though they missed their husbands very much, could not help feeling that the sacrifices they were making in being separated from them were amply justified by the results, which promised years and years of future happiness, unspoiled by the fearful sound of the tread of Roman soldiers patrolling the city, or the hoof beats of their horses. They would be free! And for this they were willing to be lonely for a few months, together with so many other wives.

Rufus, Simon's boy, was able to go to school again and learn about the past of his people, for there was no longer any Tinnius around to prevent this. Each afternoon he would come home and ask his mother for the latest about his father, postponing everything else and receiving the news with every bit of his attention, for he missed him just as much as she did, and actually counted each day since the last time he saw him. He tried hard to understand, both at school and at home, what this war was about, and sometimes he could even feel there was a good reason for it, but most of the time it was hard for him to believe that anything at all in the world was reason enough for his not seeing and talking with his own father every day.

There was an evening he missed him so much he could not even go on with his dinner. Leah, sitting opposite him, noticed him hanging his head and not eating at all.

"What is it, Rufus?" she asked anxiously. "Aren't you hungry?"

"Not very," he admitted.

"But you have only a few mouthfuls left. Why don't you finish eating and then you can go out and play again. There's still about an hour yet before the sun goes down."

"I don't want to play!" he answered.

When she heard this, she realized there must be something very wrong, for she couldn't remember when he didn't want to run outside right after dinner and play with some of the other boys. She stood up, went over to him, put her arm around his shoulder, and asked, "What *is* it, Rufus? Something must be bothering you. Did you have a fight in school?"

"No, Mother, I didn't." Finally, comforted by her closeness, he looked up at her, his mouth trembling as if he were about to cry. "Mother, when will Father be back again?"

She stared down at him, and for a few moments couldn't think of an answer which would really cheer him up. The truth was, of course, that she herself didn't know the answer, for wars were strange things: some lasted for a few days, and others raged for years.

But some sort of reply she had to give him, because already his eyes were growing moist, and silence, leaving him to imagine the worst, didn't improve matters. So she gave him a little hug and said, "Rufus, you must be very patient. Up to now our army has had miraculous success on the battlefield, and I know you are very proud of Father for being at the very head of it. Soon, when our country is free again, he will come back, and what a wonderful celebration we will have then!"

He smiled, and her heart felt warmed, grateful that her words had had this effect.

"Will I be eleven years old when he comes back?"

"Well, let's see. How old are you now?"

"Ten years and eight months."

"Yes, you may be eleven by then, or maybe even a month or two younger."

He hesitated, lowering his eyes, and she tried to guess what was going through his mind. When he looked at her again, he asked, "If I am eleven by the time he gets back . . ."

"Yes, Rufus," she encouraged him.

"Will I look the same at eleven as I do now—will he recognize me?"

She threw back her head and burst into a very free and open laugh, hugging him again.

"Of course he will! I'm sure he thinks of you every day."

"He does?"

"Yes, he does. And of me too. Both of us." He picked up his spoon and she smiled. "Ah! You're getting hungry again." But he laid it down again almost immediately.

"No, Mother." He stood up and faced her. Tall for his age, he was almost as tall now as she.

"I miss him so, Mother. We used to play so much together—he'd tell me stories—"

She made as if to embrace him again, but he stepped back from her abruptly, and suddenly he looked to her more like a man, like his father, rather than the little boy, close to tears, he had been just a minute ago.

"I know," she murmured. "You love him very much."

He looked out the window.

"The sun is coming out again. Maybe I'll go out to play for a while after all."

Her eyes shone.

"You want to now, don't you? That means you're in a better mood!"

"Yes, Mother, I am. You made me feel—we'll both be seeing Father soon."

He turned and left. She walked to the window and watched him go over to one of the children in the street and begin a game. How she longed for the war to be over and all the men to be back with their families! "You must be very patient," she had told Rufus. She bowed her head and closed her eyes. Easy advice to give, but not so easy to follow!

Chapter Twelve

At last the day, so long awaited, came. Not a single Roman remained in all of Judea! Tinnius and Publius, in spite of their best efforts and using the cleverest tricks they could think of, had been flung across the border, their troops in full flight. Once again Hadrian had to be informed of a shameful defeat at the hands of a subject people, and it was a difficult message to send, as well as to receive.

But it was a happy moment indeed for Simon when, with Eli on one side of him and Rabbi Akiba on the other, he faced a gathering of his soldiers in an open field near the Syrian border. Of course there were so many of them they could not all hear him, for there were no microphones in those days, but what he said moved back quickly by word of mouth from one row to another.

"Soldiers of Israel," he announced, "we have beaten the Romans at last!"

A great roar of triumph burst from thousands of throats, echoing backwards again and again as the announcement spread. It would have gone on for minutes if Simon had not raised his hand, for he had more—much more—to say.

"We are going to establish a State of Israel," he went on, Akiba nodding approval beside him. "This will mean that we will be free to rule ourselves and protect our country from all those who would make slaves of us. Our high priest, Rabbi Eleazar, will rededicate the altar in Jerusalem, and once more, as in the old days before we were invaded, we will be able to worship God, obey His laws and bring up our children just exactly as we see fit."

Another cheer surged like thunder from the throng, and again Simon raised his hand for silence. "And now Rabbi Akiba, without whom we could not have won, has something to say to you."

Akiba thanked him and stepped forward. "Soldiers," he told them in a firm voice, "I have prayed with all my heart and all my soul for this moment. Let us now turn our thoughts to God in gratitude for what He has done for us." He closed his eyes and intoned, "Lord, we thank Thee for this great victory, and for sending us your Messiah to make it possible. Let us, in time to come, always remember the costly sacrifices which have been made in order to free our country, and try to be worthy of them, for we lean toward forgetfulness, and soon take our most precious treasures—yes, even liberty—for granted." For a few moments he stood there, his eyes still closed, and those many thousands of men, out of respect, remained silent too. Simon cast a sidelong glance at him. "What a magnificent old man!" he thought; a man who looked as though a little passing wind would make him sway, but who found such strength within his spirit that he could defy an empire.

Akiba opened his eyes at last, and this time they were twinkling. He pointed to the pouch at Simon's waist.

"My sons," he asked with a smile, "do you know what our general carries there?"

"No!" cried one. "What do you have there, Simon?"

Simon smiled too, removed the pouch and poured its contents into his left hand. They were bright coins which sparkled warmly in the pleasant sunshine. Choosing one, he tossed it playfully into the crowd. A man seized it and inspected it closely.

" 'Simon bar Kochba—Prince of Israel,' " he read aloud, and showed it to some of his interested neighbors.

"These are examples of our new coins—they were made last week, when I was sure we would win," Simon explained. "They will be the official coins of Israel, for who ever heard of a country without money of its own?" He watched the man examining the coin eagerly and asked, "What do you think of it?"

"Beautiful!" one called and was about to pass it back, but Simon advised him, "Keep it and show it to your children!"

Another asked, "When do we go back to Jerusalem?"

"Some of you, of course, must remain here to guard our borders, but these will be relieved from time to time to go home. We must still have an army, for I have no doubt Rome will try to counterattack, and we must always be ready. Most of you, however, will see your families very soon, for you have done a splendid job, and surely deserve your reward."

A third cheer, just as wildly jubilant as the others, went up, and then he dismissed them, and turned to the Rabbi and Eli.

"How happy they are!" Eli exclaimed, watching them move back to their quarters.

"And why shouldn't they be?" asked Simon. "They

are all going home, sooner or later. We've been fighting for about a year, many of them with almost no rest.''

"They are fine men," said Akiba, "and I am very proud of every one of them!"

In a few days the soldiers returned to Jerusalem in triumph. As soon as they entered the city, the inhabitants greeted them with singing, dancing and great rejoicing. Wine flowed like water. Then the order came from Simon to break ranks, and they said goodbye to each other and made for their homes. It was a day of numberless reunions—of strange minglings of tears of welcome and rollicking laughter.

Simon had to keep himself from running as he came near his house. After all, he told himself, he was a general who had commanded about half a million men in a very tough struggle, and it would not look dignified to be seen dashing through the streets like a boy eager to get home from school. And yet he could not keep himself from walking just as fast as he could, for no man in his army was more anxious to see his family again than he.

At last he was on his own street, and though he had other things on his mind, he couldn't help taking a look around as he raced along. How odd and unfamiliar it seemed after a year of being away from it! Nothing had really changed, but somehow everything appeared different. The shops were still there, and so were the houses. And he recognized a little girl, a neighbor—though of course she was now a bit bigger—who stared at him in a puzzled way as if she didn't quite remember him, though he had often talked and joked with her.

Then he heard steps and glanced up, and there, rushing toward him with no thought at all of dignity, were Leah and Rufus.

"Leah!" he whispered as he embraced her, and then he grabbed Rufus and could only say, "Rufus!" Yet these two words seemed to say it all, at least until they had walked back together into their house and were ready for a second and better look at each other.

"Father, will you live here now?" asked Rufus.

"Yes, for a long time, I hope."

He sat down at the table and scanned the room.

"You haven't changed anything," he told Leah.

"No. Did you want me to?"

"No, it's perfect! That means it will take me less time to feel at home again."

She chuckled.

"Don't you feel at home right now?"

"Not yet," he had to admit jovially, promising, "but I will very soon. Rufus," he said, turning to him, "what are you doing these days? Going to school?"

"Yes, Father."

"That's fine. You know, those Romans wanted to close down all our schools, or change them altogether and teach you only what they wanted you to know. You wouldn't have liked that, would you?"

"No, Father. The teacher was talking to us about that just the other day. He said you and your men were fighting so that we Jews could go on studying our Law."

Simon, highly flattered, laughed.

"Did he say that? Did he really say that?"

"Yes, he did."

"And what did the class say to *that?*"

"One boy said that if not for you and Rabbi Akiba, we would all have to become just like the Romans."

"And what would be so terrible about that?"

Rufus hesitated, frowning a little, for this needed some extra thinking.

"It would be terrible because then we'd be cruel, too, and Jews are kind—or at least try to be."

Simon reached over and gave him a pat on the back.

"A good answer! I see you've been really paying attention in your class. You see, Son, we have a whole language and culture and religion of our own to pass on to our children, and if all of that is lost, I think the world would be a smaller, a lesser place. Not only that, but—" Noticing a look on Leah's face, he stopped, grinned, and remarked to her, "Or is this beginning to sound like a lecture?"

She smiled back. "I'm only wondering whether Rufus . . ."

"Understands?"

"I understand!" Rufus shouted with such certainty that his parents laughed outright with pride.

"You really do, don't you?" said Simon.

"When I grow up, I'll have a son too, and he'll go to school and learn what I'm learning, and then he'll also know why it is a better thing to be a Jew than a Roman."

"You're very clever to be able to put it that way. Some of my grown-up friends couldn't put it any better." Suddenly he rattled the new coins in his pouch.

"What's that?" asked Rufus, puzzled.

"Give me your hand."

Rufus did so, and in a few moments it filled almost to overflowing with the newly struck money. With his other hand he turned them over and over, his eyes fairly bulging out of his head.

"It says here you're a prince!" he read. " 'Simon bar Kochba—Prince of Israel.' Look, Mother!" And he chose one to give her. She examined it carefully and returned it to him. "Aren't you proud?"

"Yes, of course I am, Rufus."

He stared up at her.

"You don't *seem* very proud!"

She smiled.

"I'm sorry I don't, because I know I should be. It's only that . . ."

"What is it, Leah?" asked Simon. "Aren't they pretty enough for you?"

"Yes, they're very lovely, but I was just thinking that —well, aren't we moving ahead a bit too fast? After all, the army has just returned, we have just driven out the Romans from our country and already we have a— Prince of Israel. What does Rabbi Akiba think of your new title, by the way?"

"He approves!"

"Does he? Did he actually say he does?"

"No," he had to admit at length. "But he considers me a Messiah, a descendant of David. That is as good as being a prince, or even a king."

She shook her head.

"I am so afraid we may begin making the same mistakes the Romans made."

"You mean you're afraid I'll become just as much of a tyrant as Tinnius ever was?" he asked, looking amused. As she did not answer, he stood up and put his arm around her, holding her close to him. "You are a woman, Leah, and you worry too much. Let us enjoy our victory to the full, for it is a priceless gift from God. The Romans may give us some trouble again, but in the meantime this day, these weeks are ours. Come now, I want to see you smile. Smile! It's an order from a general!" he laughed.

She obeyed, resting her head on his shoulder. Rufus came up to them and embraced them both.

"Yes, Prince," she whispered with mock dutifulness, and they all chuckled.

Next afternoon they went to the rededication of the altar by the high priest Eleazar. Rabbi Akiba was there too, of course, as well as thousands of people from Jerusalem and the nearby villages. It was a ceremony for history to record, for it meant that once again the Jews could call their souls their own and worship God in exactly the way they saw fit, with no Tinnius to ride up and order the replacement and even destruction of everything they held dear and holy.

It was a solemn, impressive event. The aged Eleazar, garbed in the traditional headdress, breastplate and blue robe of his office, chanted his prayers with a slight tremor in his voice, as if no one knew better than he the full significance of the rite.

Soon enough it was over, and Simon and his family stayed to chat with some of their neighbors. Men who had served under him as soldiers—and were still ready to be called on—greeted him warmly as they passed by, and he waved back with equal warmth and friendliness.

Then he walked home with his wife and son, discussing the occasion with them. Yesterday had been a day of great rejoicing, but today was one rather of seriousness and taking stock.

Tinnius and Publius, though licking their wounds like whipped animals, had not at all given up hope of recapturing Judea. It was a matter, they thought, of getting still more reinforcements. Besides, Publius reasoned that if a new general could be persuaded to join them, their chances for a successful counterattack would be that much better, for if two heads were better than one, three were better than two.

Camped now in the southern part of Syria, just north of Judea, they wondered which Roman general could best know how to handle Bar Kochba, who had proven such a terrifyingly powerful opponent that only the best military brains in the Roman Empire could hope to make any headway against him.

"I know!" cried Publius suddenly. "Julius Severus!"

"Julius Severus?" repeated Tinnius. "But he is in Britain and badly needed there."

"Not so badly as he is needed here. Bar Kochba is an expert in fighting in caves and secret places—and if you will remember, that is just the kind of experience Julius has had. If we can persuade Hadrian to order him to join us, the three of us would plan such blows as the history of Rome has never known!"

Tinnius shook his head.

"I don't know whether Hadrian, after what has already happened, would—" He stopped, considering the suggestion further. The more he thought about it, the better it seemed to get. At last he agreed. "It's certainly worth a try. Let's send a messenger—"

"No messenger! This is too important a mission for anybody but ourselves."

And so it was decided that they go in person to Hadrian in Rome and present their request. They left Cornelius and other seasoned centurions in charge of their troops, with instructions to continue training them and keep them in shape, and soon were on their way.

Hadrian, noted for swift decisions, listened to the two commanders and almost immediately accepted Julius Severus as the man, if there indeed was such a one in all the world, who would be able to turn the tables on the new Prince of Israel and inflict on him a resounding and unforgettable defeat. He chose Tinnius to go to Britain with his message, while Publius returned to his troops in Syria with the cheering word that they would be joined before long by the greatest general in the Roman Empire, and then the Jews would indeed be lost.

"You will see," he assured them. "Little Judea will be ours again, and Simon bar Kochba will be very sorry he ever left his sandal maker's shop to proclaim himself a Messiah!"

Chapter Thirteen

Julius Severus, a strong-looking man in his early fifties, sat in his favorite chair in his quarters. Not so long ago he had put down a small uprising of the native Britons, and he was going over in his mind what he had learned in this maneuver, in case another revolt sprang up suddenly in another part of the country. He was the sort of officer who never really left his work, for he spent almost every spare moment studying it and trying to improve his service to Hadrian.

A soldier came in, and Julius looked up.

"Yes? What is it?"

"You have a visitor from Rome, sir—Tinnius Rufus."

"Tinnius Rufus?"

"That's right, sir—with Publius Marcellus of Syria he has been fighting the Jews."

Julius nodded.

"I've heard of that battle. How has it been going?" He frowned and stood up suddenly, squaring his shoulders. "Can it be that . . ." An idea of the object of Tinnius's visit had occurred to him, and it did not please him. "Show him in!" he finished gruffly.

"Yes, sir."

The soldier wheeled around and marched out. In a moment Tinnius appeared. They greeted each other cordially enough, and Tinnius soon came to the point.

"Julius, I have been sent by Hadrian. Have you heard of our—difficulties in Judea?"

The other smiled.

"Yes, but some of the details are missing. Have they —driven you from Jerusalem yet?"

"Worse than that—from Judea," Tinnius had to admit, crestfallen.

Julius's features darkened.

"From Judea!" he repeated, truly surprised.

"Yes. That is why I am here. Hadrian wants you to join us at the border and all three of us will plan a counter-attack." He forgot his feeling of humiliation for a few moments, and his eyes filled with delighted anticipation of what the future might hold for them. "Fighting side by side, you and I and Publius—why, we would recapture all of Judea in a matter of weeks! Why, he's just a—"

Julius waved him into silence.

"Hold on! Are you sure Hadrian knows as well as he should the situation here in Britain? If I left now, there's no telling what would happen!"

"We've all considered that, and the Emperor's decision, like ours, is that it is a risk worth taking. You can leave some of your fine centurions in command—"

Another wave, and Tinnius was silent again.

"I know the procedure I must follow." He shook his head. "When I return here, so much trouble may have brewed in my absence, it might take months before things are normal again."

"Then you'll come!" exclaimed Tinnius happily.

"Have I a choice?" he replied with a shrug. "Hadrian has issued his orders, and I must obey. And now," he added sternly, "tell me the sort of fighting this—this Bar —what's his name?"

"Bar Kochba."

"—this Bar Kochba has been doing, so that we may learn how to defeat him at his own game."

"Certainly, sir."

They sat down and before very long Julius had a clear idea of just how Simon had been able to push back two able Roman generals to the point that a third had to be called in to rescue the first two. He also learned of Simon's regarding himself as a Messiah, and how the Jews flocked behind him by the hundreds of thousands to make his mission a success. And Julius was no fool: he knew that such beliefs helped win victories just as much as fast horses and a through mastery of cave–to–cave fighting. Thus, by the time the two men joined Publius on the border of Judea, he was able to show them how to make plans for an attack on Kabul, a little village in the North.

Publius, too, was thrilled at getting so great a help as the foremost Roman general, and the word spread swiftly among the troops that Julius had arrived at last, and from now on things would be very different.

At last the counterattack was launched, and slowly the little village gave way once again to the invaders. A messenger to Jerusalem was dispatched, and Simon was soon informed that the Jewish holiday was over, and that steps had to be taken immediately to throw back the Romans. He sounded the alarm, and the many soldiers who had returned to their homes gathered anew under his leadership.

Thus it meant goodbye again to Leah and Rufus, and not much time for saying it either. He explained what had happened, and Leah was grateful for at least the few weeks he had spent with them.

"I'll be back soon!" he promised Rufus. "In the meantime, be a good boy in school and a fine son to your mother."

Rufus found it hard to hold back his tears.

"But Father," he protested, "you said you would live here now!"

"Yes, I did, but when the Romans start fighting again, I must be there to beat them back once more. Don't you understand that?"

The boy nodded.

"Yes, Father." And he added suddenly, "But why must it always be you? Don't we have any other generals?"

Simon smiled.

"They trust me. They know I have brought victory to them before, and they are sure that only I can do it again. You should be proud of their confidence!"

"Yes, Rufus, your father is only—" Leah began, but the boy interrupted:

"I *am* proud, It's just that I'd rather he lived here all the time, than just be somebody I hear about in the classroom and from you!"

Simon embraced him.

"I know how you feel, my son," he told him. "And I'm going to miss you too. But if I stayed home, there's no telling what would happen. Why, the Romans might be back patrolling our streets in two weeks. Tinnius would be back in his palace, and things would be just as bad as they were in the old days—maybe even worse. Is *that* what you would like to see?"

Rufus pressed his head against him.

"No, of course not," he answered in a muffled voice.

"All right, then—now, let's see how brave you can look." Simon reached out, gripped his shoulders and held him erect. Rufus raised his chin, set it, and looked directly into the other's eyes, trying to feel as tough as a Jewish soldier. "Fine! That's the way I want to remember you when I think of you and Mother." He turned to her and continued, "You must be brave too."

"I'll try, Simon," she promised, but he could tell by the way she answered that she was not far from tears either.

At last he was out of the house and on his way to Eli and the thousands of patriots he would lead at Kabul. It was so hard to leave his family! And yet many others were doing the same thing, and that thought itself was a kind of comfort and consolation. He wasn't the only one now who had to make a sacrifice of this sort—give up his present happiness to earn a future one. Rufus and that brave little face he had so manfully made! It was to stay in his memory a long, long time throughout the most difficult days ahead.

As they galloped north toward the captured village, Simon discussed with Eli the report that a new general, Julius Severus, had joined Tinnius and Publius.

"He is far better than the other two," Eli was sure. "Do you think we ought to—make special plans?"

"Yes, I know his reputation for what he has done in Britain," Simon nodded. "We will have to call on every trick of battle we have ever used or even heard of."

"You—you don't think there is a chance that . . ."

"That what?"

"That he will drive us back to Jerusalem."

Simon stared at him.

"Have you been worrying about such a possibility? . . . Don't answer—I can see you have!" he almost shouted. "I'm surprised at you."

Eli bowed his head a little.

"I'm sorry. But I've heard so much about him, I can't help—" He stopped again.

"Worrying," Simon suggested.

"Yes."

"You don't really have much confidence in me, do you?"

"You're wrong about that," the aide protested. "I have every confidence in the world in you! I believe you are our—Messiah."

"If you truly believe that, Eli—I mean with all your heart and mind—then why these doubts, this fear that the great general from Britain will send us scurrying for our caves?" As there was no answer, he went on, "No, my friend, I face Julius with the same spirit I faced Tinnius and then Publius. God has sent me to deliver Israel from its enemies, and certainly He did not mean to deliver it for just a little while, but forever. Yes, Julius may be a bit cleverer than the others, but he is still fighting against God's purpose, and in a contest like that no man can hope to win." His mood changing suddenly, he gave a short laugh, reached over and gave the other's back a playful, reassuring pat which was so vigorous it almost amounted to a blow. "No, don't you fret any more about this—this gnat. We will rout him from Judea just as quickly as we routed his allies!"

Eli smiled, for Simon's confidence was something which spread easily to other men, and he himself was no exception.

Yet this faith of Simon's in his mission to keep Israel

free did not seem to be enough in the coming weeks, for Kabul fell at last, and so did three and then four other nearby strongholds. Julius, it soon became clear to both Simon and Eli, was trying some new techniques, and they were working. For one thing, he used the siege, surrounding and thus trapping a fortress and cutting off its precious lifelines of supplies, so that soon the soldiers within it lacked food, water and arrows, and had to surrender. For another, Julius, assisted by Tinnius and Publius, led surprise cavalry attacks against small bodies of Jewish troops, encircling and destroying them. And finally, they no longer troubled to take their prisoners back to Syria—from their own viewpoint, they saved a lot of time and manpower by putting all their prisoners to death at once.

These three new methods of waging warfare—new to the Jews but old to Julius, who had used them with great success in Britain—were equally effective in Judea, and Simon felt himself being hurled back as if by an avalanche.

Discouraged and deeply puzzled by this sad and unexpected turn of events, he discussed it with Rabbi Akiba, who had joined him again on the front.

"Why are we losing the ground we have gained at so great a cost?" the Rabbi asked.

"I do not know," Simon had to admit, shaking his head. "I understand, of course, that he has these new tricks he has brought here from Britain, but—"

"Tricks?"

Simon explained the siege, the sudden attacks against small bodies of troops, and the immediate putting to death of all prisoners. It was the last measure which really shocked Akiba.

"The killing of all prisoners!" he exclaimed in horror.

"Yes. This saves them the trouble of escorting them back to Syria, and the soldiers who would have had to do this can be sent instead against us."

"I see. Is there no limit to their inhumanity?"

"In war there is little humanity."

Akiba stared darkly at him.

"Do you justify their executing our prisoners? Even in warfare there should be some rules of decent behavior. *We* don't kill *their* prisoners, do we?"

"No, Rabbi, we don't. Still," he considered, "since they are doing this to us . . ."

"I forbid it! We are not animals, but human beings defending our right to live in the country of our forefathers!"

Simon nodded.

"I knew you'd feel that way, Rabbi. But we are being pushed back so fast and so far, one thinks of . . . no, of course you are right. We must act better than they do, or we lose something—something which makes us different from them, and therefore more deserving to win."

Akiba smiled.

"I am very glad to hear you say that, my son. It shows me that this revolt has not taken the fear of God out of your heart, that you still remember our laws."

"Yes, I remember them, but will our children if Jerusalem and the rest of the country falls under the Roman heel again?"

The smile disappeared slowly.

"You—you think there is a chance of that?"

"As a general, I must face all possibilities, even the worst ones. The Romans, under their new leadership, *are* making astonishing headway."

"But you are learning their methods, aren't you?

Therefore you should be able to plan some ways of hitting back at them." A thought came to him. "Simon, tell me the truth! Those old doubts you had about your being—the Messiah; are they returning? You recall Leah came to me—"

"Yes, I recall very well. No, they are not returning, Rabbi. I still believe very deeply in my mission to save our people from Roman tyranny."

"But if we are being driven back, it would be only natural for you to feel that God is no longer with us."

"Yes, we are being driven back, but the war is not yet over!" was the valiant answer. "This may be just a way of testing our faith. We must prove more firmly than ever how much we believe in Him by fighting as if our setbacks are only accidents, and that tomorrow will bring us greater victories than ever!"

The Rabbi smiled again and put his hand on his shoulder.

"Spoken like a true Messiah!" he congratulated him. "God tests our faith with troubles and misfortunes, and it is only the fool and the weakling who abandon Him at the first sign of a cloud."

Chapter Fourteen

In spite, however, of Simon's growing skill in predicting just where Julius would strike next, and Akiba's constant fervent prayers for the success of the Jewish forces, the Romans continued to advance into Judea, seizing one stronghold after another as if they were pears falling from a ripe tree. Nothing Simon's patriots could do was able to hold them back, though they fought just as boldly and heroically as ever. It just seemed as if the time of their success had run out, and it was the Romans' turn to win.

Before long Jerusalem itself was taken, and this was a blow which many of its inhabitants accepted as a sign of the complete defeat which had to come. But the Jewish army continued to struggle gallantly, making the enemy pay dearly for every precious inch of ground it regained.

Leah and Rufus, of course, mourned the fall of their city as bitterly as their neighbors, but tried to be as brave as they could, for they knew that was the way Simon wanted it. She still owned their shop, but since she was not at all skilled in the making of sandals, like her husband, she used it for the mending of garments. And Rufus, after school was over, would play for a while and then join her, helping her in any way he could.

When the Roman patrols passed in the street, either on foot or on horseback, mother and son would exchange glances which said, "Soon! You will see. Simon will be back and chase these wretched invaders out of the country again—this time for good! We must be patient and courageous."

Yet some of her customers lost hope quickly, and even got used to the presence of the Romans. One, for example—an elderly lady named Hannah—went as far as to blame Simon for causing his people a lot of trouble by starting the revolt in the first place. She came into the shop one morning, picked up her robe and paid for its mending. One her way out she stopped at the door. Leah was there alone, for Rufus was still in his class. "Have you heard from your great husband lately?" she asked, turning.

If she had just said, "Have you heard from your husband lately?" without using the word "great," Leah would have answered simply, "No. In these times messages from our warriors are hard to deliver and receive." But there was a kind of bite in that word, and Leah knew that Hannah meant Simon was not great at all, but only pretended to be.

She tried to control her temper, and for a few moments said nothing.

"No, I have not," she managed at last.

Hannah smiled, and it was not a friendly smile.

"He's probably too busy running for his life to bother sending you any messages!" she taunted.

This was too much to bear, and Leah cried, "He is

fighting for his life, and for yours too, if you only had the common sense to see it!''

The other took a step toward her.

"Fighting for *my* life?" she asked, sincerely puzzled. "I am living well enough, and so is my—"

"Yes, living! Only because the Romans decide to let you. But suppose you wanted to study our Law, observe our Sabbath—would they let you live then?"

The customer shrugged.

"If your husband hadn't begun this stupid rebellion, Hadrian would probably have changed his mind sooner or later, and revoked his edicts. Simon has only made matters worse by—"

"Out!" Leah shouted. "Out of my shop, you silly woman!"

Hannah, frightened by this outburst, turned back to the door, opened it and scurried out with the speed of a mouse. For a few minutes Leah was so upset by her words that she could do nothing but sit down and try to compose herself. To think that there was even one person in Jerusalem who could feel this way about what Simon had done! Of course Hannah would not be back with other work for her, but it didn't matter. There were others who really understood and appreciated the reasons for a fierce struggle to live in freedom and peace, and had the intelligence to honor those who led such a struggle.

But Hannah was not the only one who stopped coming to Leah's shop. She had friends, and spread the word among them that Leah, screaming like a wild woman, had driven her out. And she urged them to take their trade elsewhere. Her advice, when falling on ears as foolish and misguided as her own, was often followed, and Leah noticed it became harder and harder for her to manage.

Even Rufus felt the difference between having a victorious hero for a father and a retreating general. His classmates no longer mentioned Simon to him, nor treated the boy as anything special. In fact, it was a painful subject all around, for when it happened that they would talk of their own parents, comparing them proudly, one might face Rufus and begin, "And what about your—" and then stop, remembering who Simon was, and dropping his eyes in embarrassment.

Since Hadrian's edicts no longer permitted the Jews to study their own laws, the teachers had to be very careful in referring to the revolt, for if they made it sound as if it were a just one, and somehow word of this got back to the Romans, there was no telling how far they would go in punishing them: even death was possible.

Rufus had a friend, Samuel, who had been especially thrilled and excited when Simon was driving the enemy out of the country. And even now, when the tables were turned, he remained very close, always asking him for news of his father, and following the battles, as reports of them drifted back to Jerusalem, with the keenest interest.

One day, however, Rufus noticed that he was very distant, did not smile at him, and hardly greeted him. This puzzled him very much, but he thought that maybe his friend was having a bit of trouble at home, and so he did not let the matter bother him. In a day or two, he was sure, Samuel would be his usual sunny, chummy self again.

But when two days passed—and then three—and Samuel still hardly said a single word to him, Rufus knew that something was very wrong. One afternoon he called after him as they were leaving school, "Samuel!"

The boy turned, and for a moment his eyes lit up and he smiled, but then instantly, as if he recalled something, his face became grave again and he turned away. Rufus broke into a run and caught up with him.

"Samuel!" he repeated. "What's the matter?"

"Nothing," was the mumbled answer.

He began hurrying down the street toward his home, Rufus following.

"Nothing! But there must be *some*thing," he insisted.

Samuel stopped and looked at him squarely.

"Rufus," he began, his voice sounding a little strange. And he could not go on.

His friend grabbed his arm.

"What is it? *Tell* me!" he demanded.

"The—the other boys . . ."

"The other boys? What about them?" A thought came to him, and he took his hand away. It just didn't seem possible. Could it be that— And yet the question had to be asked. "Samuel, have they been telling you not to— talk to me any more?"

Samuel dropped his eyes to the ground, and then abruptly nodded.

"Yes," he said faintly.

"But why? You mean because of . . ." There could be no other explanation. "Because my father . . ."

Samuel looked at him directly again.

"Yes, it's about your father. Oh, sometimes I hate them!" he burst out. "When things were going well, and all the soldiers came home, and the temple was rededicated, everybody thought your father was a great man, a real Messiah! But now, just because things are *not* going so well any more, and Jerusalem is a Roman city again, everybody starts turning against him."

"Everybody?" repeated Rufus quietly. "I haven't. My mother hasn't."

"I mean the boys in class. And some of their parents too, if you must know."

Rufus wondered what he could say next. For a moment he was close to tears, but he succeeded in holding them back manfully. Wasn't it enough that he never saw his own father any more—did his classmates have to reject him also, even go as far as to make a very good friend join them in their cruel silence?

A spirit of angry protest suddenly welled in him.

"Why do you listen to them? Are you afraid of them?" He nodded grimly. "That's it," he accused. "You're afraid of them!"

"No, I'm—" the other began, but could not go on, for he had been brought face to face with his own fears. "Yes," he had to admit at last, unable to meet Rufus's eyes. "They frighten me. They told me they'd . . ."

"What?"

"They said if I talked to you any more, they'd start treating me just as they treat you."

"And that would be a terrible thing, wouldn't it? In other words, you'd rather have them for friends, and hide your feelings about my father, than stay friends with me and *show* them."

Samuel's face brightened.

"I have an idea!" he exclaimed. "Why don't we meet outside of school some time, and then we can go on being chums, but as long as we're in school—"

Rufus's darkening expression stopped him.

"You mean in school you'd act one way and outside another."

"You—you don't think it's such a good idea?" he faltered.

"It's awful!" he burst out. "Either you're a friend of mine, or you aren't, and it doesn't make a bit of difference whether we're in school, in the street, in a shop, in your home or mine, or any other place!" He seemed to get angrier with each word, so that by the time he finished, he was a very red-faced and furious boy indeed. And then, as if in a single moment there were no words left in him at all, he turned and ran home.

Leah was at the shop now, and therefore he did not have to worry very much about how he looked, for he was sure that if she could see him, she would have a dozen questions to ask him, such as "What happened?", "Where have you been?", "Why are you so red?" and so on. He went into the house and got himself some fruit to eat, but could not take his mind away from the scene in the street. He tried to tell himself that none of this really mattered, that Samuel wasn't such a wonderful person to know, or else why did he act so cowardly? But no matter what he told himself, the hurt was still there, and he wished with all his soul that the war were over, and his father were home to make everything right again. Then his classmates would be proud to talk to him, and so would Samuel!

But his father was far away, strengthening his position in Bethar, the very last fortress left to him in all of Judea, and there was no way really of knowing when he would be home again. One by one the villages and towns had fallen under the Roman advance, till only Bethar remained. Yet somehow the spirit of the soldiers under Simon's command still flamed with defiance and rebellion, for wasn't he the Messiah, and hadn't he been sent by God Himself to make their country their own again?

Realizing he must now prepare himself for a long siege, Simon used every device he could think of to make the enemy pay dearly for each second it spent camped outside the city. The arrows at his disposal were by now quite limited in number, and each one had to find a mark, for there were none to waste. Stones, boulders—anything which could possibly be hurled into the effort to keep the Romans from breaking in—were gathered against the day the ammunition ran out. Some men were even put to work building new arrows with whatever suitable materials could be found. Oddly enough, very few grumbled as yet about their retreat, for, besides being kept strong by their great faith in Simon, they were all far too busy to be worrying about what might happen to them. It was their relatives who were *not* in the army who really fretted and easily gave up hope, for they had more time to think, and therefore complain.

Simon, looking a bit older but as firmly convinced as ever of the righteousness of their revolt, and therefore of its eventual triumph, strode about through all the bustling activity around him—directing, commanding, suggesting, even joking. No wonder his soldiers obeyed him! He was a man not only to listen to and admire, but to love. Often he would join them in their labors, considering none of the jobs to be beneath his dignity, for didn't each one of them point in exactly the same direction—victory?

Once, on one of his tours of the besieged city, he noticed a heavy-set youth working alone on a kind of personal fort, building up a barricade of rocks till it was up to his eyes! This was nothing very unusual in itself, but there was a kind of swiftness and sureness about him and, more than that, an air of the greatest concentration, as if no task on earth could possibly be more important or hold more interest.

Simon did not know the young man's name—in fact, did not even remember ever having seen him before, since there were many thousands serving under him, and he couldn't know everybody. But he had to stop and watch this fellow in particular. It soon seemed to him he could have stood there an hour without the other's becoming aware that he was being closely observed and scrutinized by his top commander.

At length, with a smile, Simon took a couple of steps and stood right next to him. Looking up at him at last, the man recognized him and immediately sprang to attention.

Simon, his smile broadening, patted his back and said, "Relax. What are you doing here?"

"Building a fort, sir!" And he added with a grin, "The way things are going, I might have to use it."

Simon nodded.

"We *are* in a bad spot, aren't we?"

"Yes, sir." He went on boldly, "But we've been in worse spots before, and pulled through. We'll pull through this one also!"

Simon said nothing for a few moments.

"What is your name?" he asked at length.

"Ithamar."

"Have I ever spoken to you before?"

"No, sir. I haven't had that honor."

"It is I who haven't had the honor, my friend. You're one of my bravest, and I'm proud of you."

Ithamar straightened till he seemed an inch or two taller, his eyes shining.

"Thank you, sir!"

Simon was about to move on, but something about the other's bearing still held him.

"You realize, of course, we might be here for a long, long time. Six months, a year—only God knows. Do you think you will be able to—endure it?"

"Yes!" was the unhesitating reply. "As long as I know there are many others who fight alongside of me and—an officer like you to lead me, I will stay here as long as I'm needed. Even the Romans can be defeated, sir—as we have already shown them!"

"Yes, we *have* shown them, haven't we?" Simon nodded again, the memory of those few happy, triumphant weeks in Jerusalem crossing his mind and for a moment almost blotting out all the dreadful defeats and retreats which followed.

"And we'll show them again!" Ithamar exclaimed so loudly and confidently that several other soldiers working nearby paused to look at him.

"Yes, we must," Simon agreed, and walked on at last. "What a spirit!" he thought. With a thousand men like him he could hold Bethar forever. . . . Ithamar. He would not soon forget that name, nor the face that went with it. And there must be so many others like him whom he had never said a single word to, whose very names were strange to him! But they were all with him, all ready to take the worst the Romans had to offer and give them back blow for blow, and more.

Chapter Fifteen

As the weeks and months passed, however, and the Romans gave no hint of abandoning the siege—in fact each day seeming to strengthen it—it was the Jews who found themselves battling desperately against one of the grimmest enemies of all—starvation. Julius Severus had proven himself once again a master of one of his old tricks—surrounding a fortress and in this way cutting off its supply lines, so that fresh food, water and arrows never reached his trapped opponents. The result, sooner or later, was surrender.

After six months of the siege, Simon knew that his men —even the toughest and most heroic of them—could not be expected to hold out much longer. Their pinched looks and short tempers were sure signs that the end was near. Soldiers who had been close friends for years suddenly found themselves in violent arguments over little things they would have ignored or even laughed off when the war was going well. But now everything, no matter how trivial, seemed to be a cause of irritation and sometimes explosive anger. No, it was a different army Simon saw around him, and he shook his head sadly and sometimes wondered whether it would not be the wiser course to give in to the Romans right away, rather than try to postpone what could not be avoided in any case.

Yet the word "surrender" itself now meant "death"—so how, was his next thought, could he seriously consider it? At least now—though famished, embittered and fighting among themselves—they were still alive, and as long as the breath of life was still in them, there was reason to hope.

When the six months dragged into seven, the grumblers began to be heard more often and more loudly. "Why are we here?" one would ask. "How could Simon dare to defy the whole Roman Empire? We must have been mad to follow him!" And yet these same harassed and starving soldiers, whose pangs of hunger rather than their minds spoke for them, could not offer a solution for their troubles, for whichever way they turned, only death faced them. All they could do was remember when there had been a chance *not* to place their faith in Simon, and deeply regret their decision to follow him.

Luckily, however, as the grumblers grew in number, so did their critics, those who still stalwartly defended every move Simon had ever made. "Fools! Cowards!" they cried. "Would you prefer now to live under the Roman heel—lick their boots, bow to their commands? At least we have shown them that if they treat us as slaves, they have a fighting army of patriots on their hands. Better by far death on a battlefield than a lifetime of slavery!"

Eli, still Simon's staunch friend and ally, was keenly aware of these flaring tempers and clashes, and often reported them to him. One afternoon, as he strode through the city, an arrow whirred past his head. He wheeled, noticed a soldier in headlong flight around a corner, raced after him, but lost him in a crowd. He approached Simon in a very angry mood, for he felt the time had certainly come for something to be done about the grumblers.

"We must threaten to punish them!" he urged fiercely. "Our life here is hard enough without having to listen to all the complaining. And that wretch who tried to kill me—he's a traitor!"

Simon, angry too, nodded.

"Of course he is—too bad you didn't catch him. We would have executed him."

"Execution—wouldn't that be too severe a punishment for those who complain?"

"On second thought, yes, and Akiba would feel that way too, I'm sure."

"But what shall we do then? For we must do *some*thing to shut them up. Grumbling is like a plague which spreads from one man to another, and in the end we may have a rebellion of our own right here in Bethar!"

"Perhaps," Simon suggested, "since it's hunger they're complaining about mostly, we will announce that each man who mentions it will be denied any food at all for twenty-four hours. Do you believe that will work?"

"I'd make it forty-eight!" Eli retorted grimly.

Simon smiled.

"I see that arrow must have taken some of the skin off your ear."

Eli raised his hand to it.

"No, but I could hear the whir as plainly as my own breathing."

Simon's smile disappeared.

"If it had happened to me, I'd have made sure to catch that man."

"But I ran after him and—" Something in the other's

eye stopped him. Yes, he thought, Simon *would* have caught him.

In the end they decided that twenty-four hours without food and water would be enough of a punishment for a soldier heard complaining. But before going ahead with the announcement, Simon considered it wise to discuss it with Rabbi Akiba—his usual practice whenever an important decision had to be made.

When the Rabbi heard of the grumblers, he was shocked. Prayers had been taking up so much of his time, this was news to him. At first he was reluctant even to believe it.

"I cannot understand," he said, "how even a few of our fine soldiers who have stood by you for so long and through so many hazards can now turn their backs on you and be sorry they ever followed you."

"They're starving," replied Simon. "When a man is hungry enough, he will sometimes change his mind about something he has never before had a single doubt about."

"Still, do you think starving him even further will make him a better soldier?"

Simon told him about the arrow incident—how Eli had narrowly escaped injury, perhaps even death.

"If we do nothing about this," he finished, "others will shoot at him too—and at me also, for that matter, for I am certainly more responsible than he for the revolt. Yes, Rabbi—some wretched, misguided culprit might even aim an arrow at *you*!"

The Rabbi reflected for a few moments, and then went on. "Why don't *I* go among them—talk to them? I see now I have been keeping too much to myself and my prayers. If I hear a man complaining . . ." He stopped.

"I don't think he would in your presence."

"If, as you say, one might even aim an arrow at me, why would he hesitate about complaining to me? No, Simon, you are wrong. Let me go among them and speak to them, for I am their Rabbi and if they are heavy of heart, it is I who must lighten it and give them fresh courage."

Simon agreed at last, and postponed his announcement about the punishment until he saw what the Rabbi might accomplish in his own way.

Immediately Akiba made a very thorough tour of the city. He saw and heard everything he could. Soldiers greeted him in the traditionally respectful manner, and for a few hours he observed nothing which justified Simon's fears. He was about to go back to his quarters when he noticed a soldier frowning at him and then turning away. He was about to move on, thinking nothing further of this, but instead decided to greet him.

"Hello, young man!" The other mumbled something in reply. "I did not hear you," Akiba added.

"Does it matter?" said the soldier, facing him slowly, and a more downcast and disheartened expression Akiba had not seen in months. Besides the usual pinched and famished look shared by every other soldier, there was a kind of deadness in the eyes, as if whatever love of life had ever gleamed in them had long since been extinguished.

The Rabbi stepped closer to him and put his hand on his shoulder.

"You are very tired, my son, aren't you?" he asked kindly.

The man glanced at the comforting hand, and for a moment Akiba was afraid it would be brushed off. But then the other looked at him again, his expression softening.

"Yes, Rabbi," he answered simply, "I am very tired," adding with a trace of humor at the corners of his eyes, "and very hungry too."

"Of course you are! So are we all."

A pleading, almost child-like expression suddenly came over the soldier's face.

"Rabbi, what will be the end of this? Are we all going to starve here like rats?"

"No!" was the firm reply. "God will deliver us."

"God," he repeated dully.

"Yes! He has sent us His Messiah, Simon bar Kochba, and Simon will surely deliver us."

The youth turned away again.

"I no longer believe this, Rabbi," he said faintly.

"What is that?" Akiba demanded, not believing his own ears. "What did you say?"

The man faced him once more.

"Look around you, Rabbi. Do you think that God will rescue us from all of this? Soon you will have to perform the funeral ceremony over some of us, for we shall certainly perish of starvation. No, Rabbi, it is clear to me that God is too busy elsewhere to be concerned about us here in little Bethar."

Such lack of faith filled the Rabbi with a great, sudden fury, for it showed him that this fellow had never really taken his religion seriously. As if God ever forgets anyone who follows His commandments! He had the impulse to seize him and make him take back his words immediately, but his truer, gentler self continued to assert itself, and he breathed heavily and said nothing for a few moments until he was completely calm again.

"My son," he answered at last, "you do not understand God and His ways. You ask me to look around."

He did so, sadly. "Yes, I see misfortune here, and great suffering, but God does not dwell only in a happy man's house. He lives also with the poor, the hurt, the discouraged. In fact, don't you see? It is *these* who need Him much more than the happy. *Now,* my friend, is the very time for you to say your prayers—more than any other." He had raised his voice a little, and now he noticed that some of the other soldiers had come closer to hear him better. "Yes, my sons," he went on, "Simon *is* our Messiah—have no doubt about that—and if you continue to show your faith in him, he will lead us out of this dark and dangerous spot to a better life than you have ever known!"

"But, Rabbi," one called out, "we are losing our strength every day! How can you tell us that—"

"Stop!" he interrupted angrily. His face working, he tried to think of the words which would best serve him at this trying moment. At last he continued, "I am ashamed. Do you hear me? Ashamed! In what way are you better than those Romans out there who seek to destroy us? They too have no faith in our one God. I tell you this is a testing place. Those who no longer believe in the Almighty will die, while those who still believe will be rescued!"

Angrily he turned and would have left them, but another soldier held him by his tunic.

"Rabbi," this man said, close to tears, "we want to believe! With all our hearts we want to have faith that God watches over us each moment of the day and night, and that He has sent Simon to deliver us. But we are only human, and our eyes see nothing before us but greater and greater defeat and hunger until we are all dead in a common grave—the believing together with the unbelieving!"

Akiba faced him squarely, for this had moved him deeply.

"My son, you are human, and so am I, and therefore, we can see little more than what is right in front of us. But I am an old Rabbi, and my thoughts have been on God's ways for many, many years. What do you know now of what the Romans are planning? You are not in their camp, but here. Perhaps, seeing that we have held out so long without surrendering, they are about to give up. *They* are mortal, too, and therefore the subjects of God's will. But if they should break in here tomorrow and seize the city, and all of us in it, I shall die happily, knowing that this is God's decision, not to be questioned by such as you and I . . . This is my faith, my son. Now what is yours?"

The soldier bowed his head, dropping his hand.

"I am sorry, Rabbi," he said. "I—I did not think."

Akiba walked away again in the direction of his quarters. In a few moments he heard some grumblings behind him, rising like distant thunder, increasing with each step he took, as if his presence and words had been enough to keep them in check, but once he moved off, the restraint was gone, and complaints were free to be voiced. He had the inclination to turn and glance at them again, perhaps silencing them with just this one look, but he hurried ahead, for he had already said all he could at this time, and the rest was for them to ponder. Simon's idea about an arrow being aimed even at him crossed his mind suddenly, and for a moment he was frightened. But then he raised his chin boldly and continued walking, his step as firm as a young man's. If this was the way he was to die, a Jewish arrow in his back, that was God's decision too, and not for him to question.

Chapter Sixteen

He came back to his quarters and sat down heavily in a chair, for suddenly he felt very old and very tired indeed. What hurt him most, of course, was the thought that the soldiers were losing their faith, and for this, since he was their Rabbi, he felt himself wholly responsible. And yet how much more could he do, especially since each day made their bodies weaker, and therefore their spirits also?

He heard a step and, recognizing it as Simon's, raised his head and tried to mask his sadness with a livelier and more confident expression. It would never do to let Simon see him discouraged, for he would worry about him and take his mind away from much more pressing and important matters than the mood of an aged and weary Rabbi who belonged in any other place than a besieged city.

But Simon was not easily fooled—he could see at a glance that Akiba was not his usual self.

"What happened?" he asked concernedly. "Didn't they even bother to listen to you?" Akiba tried to struggle to his feet, but the other's firm hand on his shoulder kept him seated. "Rest!" he urged. "You do not look well. And if you prefer to talk some other time—"

Akiba managed a smile and a wave of the hand.

"Right now will be good enough. We are at war, and postponements are the luxuries of a people at peace. Yes, Simon, they listened to me, but I must admit not all of them were equally impressed by what I had to say. The—the grumblers and complainers are increasing, I'm afraid, and I agree with you now that we must do something very definite about them."

"Did any of them—threaten you?"

"No, Simon, not one. But I was talking to a group, and as I walked away, their voices rose and it seemed . . . But it may be I am exaggerating."

"It seemed they might attack you after all!"

Akiba looked at him.

"I could not really tell," he answered slowly. "But I know that some men, if pushed hard enough, will resort to desperate measures, even in regard to a person they usually admire and respect."

Simon stroked his cheek thoughtfully.

"It may be best in the future for you to stay here, Rabbi, rather than brave their anger. I should not want to—lose you."

Akiba laughed.

"You will not lose me. Nor, now that I think further about them, do I find I fear them in the least. It is *they* who are afraid—afraid of dying of hunger—while I have the love of God to sustain me even in these most difficult of times."

Eli appeared at the door.

"What is it, Eli?" Simon asked.

"There are some men outside who say they want to talk to you."

"Do you know them?"

"Some of them I do, and some I don't."

"Excuse me, Rabbi."

"Of course, my son."

He went out into the street, Eli and Akiba following, and saw about eight soldiers staring at him as if wondering just how to put into words what they had in their minds.

"You have something to tell me?" he asked.

At last one of them stepped forward. He was of medium height, dark of complexion and spoke in a firm, clear tone.

"Simon," he said, "we have come to ask you to do the one thing which would surely help us all."

"I am glad you came, for I am always interested in hearing what my men have to say. What is this thing I should do, in your opinion?"

"Surrender to the Romans before it is too late and we are all dead of starvation!"

"Surrender?" He laughed outright. "Young man, what is your name?"

The spokesman, tightening his mouth, hesitated for just a fraction of a second and then answered strongly, "Amos."

"You need not be afraid to tell me, Amos, for I myself have had the very same thought more than once." At this, the soldiers seemed to relax a little, their faces brightening and looking much less guilty and doubtful. "But Amos," he went on, "do you remember what the Romans *do* to their prisoners? Or have you forgotten so soon?"

"We have not forgotten. Do you really think, though, they would kill all of us? There are hundreds of thousands of us here. It is hard for me to believe they could be so cruel."

"They are cruel enough to make war against us in our own country! Why shouldn't they be cruel enough to destroy us all if we give ourselves over to them like sheep for slaughtering?" He shook his head. "No, surrendering to them is not the answer."

"But suppose we bargained with them!" the other insisted.

"Bargained?"

"Yes! We would promise to give up Bethar if they permitted us to lay down our arms and return to our homes in peace and safety."

Simon shook his head again, this time rather sadly.

"They would never accept such a bargain. They wish to kill us, and nothing less than that would satisfy them. From their viewpoint, we have already caused them a very great deal of trouble, and the spirit of revenge itself would force them to break any bargain they ever made with us, even if they could be drawn into one in the first place."

Amos set his jaw, and a very determined-looking young man he was.

"We could *try!*"

An answer formed in Simon's mind, but he waited a few seconds until the words fell into exactly the right place, like obedient soldiers, for he wanted to make himself perfectly clear. Besides, a kind of impatience was beginning to irritate him, and this was no time to lose one's head. How sure of himself this fellow was! And how terribly, dangerously wrong!

"You really trust our enemies, don't you?" he remarked at last, sounding as calm as if he were discussing the color of the sky. Since Amos did not say anything immediately, he went on, "Suppose we *did* make an arrangement with them, as you suggest, and they agreed to our terms, and we surrendered the city—*our very last fortress*—to them. Would you put your very life at the mercy of a man like Julius Severus, who up to now has the unspoiled record of executing every single one of his prisoners? I, for one, would not, and would sooner die by my own hand than by that of a bitter and vengeful enemy. Why, to him making a deal with us would be just another clever military trick! Don't you see that, soldier?"

Amos bowed his head slowly, half–closing his eyes as he considered this. His followers stared at him, waiting tensely for him to speak. At last he raised his head again and murmured, "Starvation is a bitter enemy too, Simon. If it were up to me . . . if I were you . . . I would risk being killed by Julius instead of facing certain death by starvation!"

Simon took a step toward him and the two men confronted each other squarely.

"I am very glad for the sake of all of us," said Simon in a slow, measured way, "that you are not in charge of this fortress. And now, my friend, have you anything further to say to me?"

Amos straightened proudly.

"No, Simon, I haven't!"

"Then back to your duties!" he ordered sharply, "and my advice is, 'Think no more of surrender,' for that is something we will never do as long as I am still in command here!"

"Yes, sir."

He wheeled, signaled to the other soldiers and they

strode back briskly to their posts. Simon's eyes remained fixed on them until they disappeared around a corner.

"Surrender!" he repeated half to himself and half to Eli and the Rabbi, and never had he used a word with more contempt.

News of the visit spread quickly throughout the city, and the men took sides just as quickly. There were those who assured Amos that he was right, and others—still by far the majority—who considered his ideas those of a traitor, and the ones who defended them traitors too. Actual fighting broke out here and there between members of the two groups, and when this was reported to Simon, he knew the time for severe disciplinary action had come.

Immediately he issued an announcement that any man who even *mentioned* the possibility of giving up to the Romans would receive no food and water for a day. Rabbi Akiba agreed to this too, realizing that when Jews began to fight among themselves, the next step would be a complete breakdown of their defense effort and certain defeat. How the Romans would have rejoiced if they knew what was going on such a short distance away within the city's walls!

For more than a week after the announcement, no Jewish soldier dared raise his voice in favor of seeking to strike a bargain with the enemy, for if the little food he was getting were denied him for a day, hunger might fell him in the streets, and the very thing he was struggling to avoid would hit him a harder blow than ever before —perhaps even a fatal one. Amos's friends were now afraid even to speak to him, lest their words be misinterpreted by some passerby and cause them to be brought before Simon for judgment. As for Amos himself, his feelings remained exactly the same, but he held his tongue and bided his time. "Let us starve a little longer," he told himself grimly. "Then more and more of us will begin to see just how wrong our great commander can be!"

One night Simon was suddenly awakened by a great, rhythmic roar right outside his quarters. At first, still half-asleep, he could not quite make out what was being shouted—almost chanted—but at last the words came through: "Surrender! Let us surrender! Surrender! Let us surrender!" He sat up, pushed his feet quickly into his sandals and dashed out into the street. It could not have been more than three or four seconds from his bed to the open air, but all he could see of the disturbance was a few backs retreating swiftly under cover of darkness.

"Eli!" he called, and his aide rushed out. "Did you recognize any of the voices?"

"No, Simon. I have a suspicion or two, but not enough to go on."

"Cowards!" he muttered. "They wouldn't have *dared* do this in daylight."

"Let's post guards—they will catch them next time, or at least a few of them, and the prisoners might be forced to give the names of the rest."

"Good idea. Still . . ."

"What?"

"It—saddens me to have to start pursuing some of my own men, good soldiers who have been so completely loyal to me through so many battles. Eli, do you think . . ."

"No, Simon," he answered, reading his mind. "Surrender is impossible, and they are fools to favor it. They must be caught and punished, just as you announced."

"Of course they must," Simon nodded grimly. "Post the guards."

This was done, and there was no further disorder that night. The very next one, however, Simon was abruptly awakened again by the sing-song bellow, this time coming not from outside his door, but from a few streets away: "Surrender! Let us surrender!" It was clear to him that someone was planning all of this, and if this fellow were not stopped, he could do a great deal of harm. Simon rushed out again and watched his guards scampering in the direction of the voices. In a minute they faded, and in another the guards returned with two captured soldiers.

"Turn them loose," he said. When they were free, he commanded them, "Step forward." They did so, one of them looking directly and proudly into Simon's eyes, and the other lowering his head as if ashamed. "You know the penalty for even mentioning the word 'surrender,' to say nothing of shouting it through the streets as if it were a battle cry?"

The proud one answered immediately, "Yes, sir!"

Simon turned to the other.

"What about you?"

"Yes, sir," he repeated in a mumble.

"Look at me!" Simon ordered. The man obeyed. Simon, taking a step toward him, saw with a twinge he could not have been more than eighteen, and badly frightened. "What made you do it?" he asked in a kinder tone, remembering that this youth was only a few years older than Rufus.

"One of the—soldiers persuaded us."

"Which one?"

His fellow captive glared at him.

"Silence!" he whispered fiercely.

Simon turned on the speaker.

"One more word out of you to him, and your sentence will be doubled!"

"Yes, sir."

Deciding on a new approach, he told the guards, "Remove this man and lock him up. No food for him for twenty-four hours! Two of you stay here."

When the soldier had been taken away, Simon faced the youth.

"Now, my son, tell me which soldier it was who persuaded you to join in the shouting." As the other hesitated he went on impatiently, "Don't you realize he is a traitor, and if you don't answer, you are shielding a traitor, and therefore no better than one yourself?"

"Y-yes, I realize it," the prisoner ventured at last.

"Then prove your loyalty to your people by giving me his name immediately, and it will surely be the wisest thing you have done in a long time!"

"His name is—Amos," he blurted, and took a deep breath, as if a great burden had suddenly slipped from his shoulders.

"Amos. You mean that same Amos who came to me a couple of weeks ago?"

The soldier nodded.

"Yes, the same."

"I see," he said thoughtfully. "Thank you." He turned to the guards. "Lock him up, but not with the other man. Give him no food for twenty-four hours."

As they marched him away, Eli ran up.

"Simon!" he exclaimed breathlessly. "The Romans have broken through! They're already fighting in our streets!"

Chapter Seventeen

Simon sounded the alarm, and soon the fiercest battle of the whole revolt raged through the streets of Bethar like a sudden thunderstorm. Each Jewish soldier felt that this was his very last chance to defend himself, and used spear and arrow with every bit of skill and strength he could summon from his aching, hungry body. The Romans had to be pushed back out of the city *now*— for tomorrow might be too late.

Simon seemed to be everywhere, giving his men courage, urging them on to even greater effort than they were already showing, exulting at each fallen Roman. But the Jews fell too, and it seemed to both sides the toll was so great that such a fearful contest could not last for long.

Yet somehow the hours passed, and morning came, and still the struggle went on, neither army ready to accept defeat. Roman horsemen kept charging murderously through the streets, slashing at the defenders of the city, while the latter aimed, dodged and thrusted as if they had been born for war and nothing else.

At one point Simon saw an opening through which he thought he and his men could push their way out of the fortress and close in on some of their enemies with an encircling, pincer-like clutch. Taking advantage of a slight lull in the fighting, he rallied them around, gave his commands and led them in this wild, desperate rush to escape Bethar, which could easily become a tomb if they stayed in it too long.

Most of them succeeded in this bold venture, but many fell. Those who remained attacked the Romans from the rear, thus forcing them to battle for their lives in two directions. However the Romans, still greatly outnumbering their enemy, were finally able to break out of this deadly embrace and inflict heavy damage. Simon fought back with all the strength left to him, but soon he saw that it was a hopeless cause. Too many of his soldiers were being cut down, and he ordered the brave survivors to race back into Judea. Hotly pursued, they hid in caves, some of them escaping capture for a week and others making their way gradually home. Simon himself was one of the unlucky ones caught.

Brought before Julius Severus in Bethar, he asked calmly, "Are you going to kill me?"

"Doesn't the fate of your fellow Jews interest you?"

"I already know it."

"Bethar is ours!" Julius proclaimed proudly. "In fact, all Judea is ours once more! Don't you regret now this foolish and impossible revolt against us?"

Simon hesitated.

"No," he answered at last.

Julius seemed puzzled.

"How can you say 'No'? Everything you have fought for has been taken from you. Even your life is no longer yours, for a word from me, and that guard standing next to you will plunge his spear through you."

"You do not understand, Julius."

The general frowned.

"No, I do not," he had to admit.

"We have proved to the world that we have a faith we are willing to risk our lives for—die for, if necessary. Besides, we had those few, glorious weeks of freedom when we'd driven you from the country. They did not last very long, but they were very sweet, and they showed what men can achieve if they are willing to fight hard enough . . . Has—has Akiba been captured too?"

"Akiba?"

"Yes, Rabbi Akiba! Have you taken him too?"

Tinnius Rufus, standing next to Julius, whispered into his ear.

"Yes," said Julius. "I am told we have."

"May I see him?"

"Why?" He smiled contemptuously. "Are you planning another rebellion?" Simon did not answer. "Very well," he went on impatiently. "You have my permission. But I must warn you: do not expect any further mercies from us. You are both our prisoners, and we make no exceptions to the rule. You are both to die before another day has passed!"

Accordingly Simon was locked in a prison, and soon the Rabbi, haggard but still erect and dignified, was brought in.

"You have only half an hour," the guard told them gruffly and left.

The two men embraced.

"Akiba!" exclaimed Simon. "It is wonderful to see you again. Tell me—have you any news of Eli?"

"He is alive, but captured too, my son. They mean to kill us all, don't they?"

"Yes, but we must be brave to the end, for if we act the coward, we shall be only making a mockery of all we have struggled for up to now, and the Romans will laugh at us."

"I do not intend to act the coward," the other assured him. "My faith is as strong as ever." Simon suddenly turned away. "What is the matter?" Akiba asked concernedly. As there was no immediate answer, he moved around so he could see him better. And still Simon avoided his eyes. "There *is* something! Why don't you tell me?"

Simon faced him at last.

"You can speak of faith now?" he said huskily.

Akiba nodded.

"I see." He looked about him. "We are standing here in this room which only yesterday was ours, but which today is a prison, and from here we shall go to our deaths for the crime of wanting to go on being Jews. This takes away something from your faith in God, doesn't it? Ah, Simon, I'm disappointed in you! Why, wasn't it you who said to me not so long ago, when the Romans had just seized Kabul in the North, as well as a few neighboring villages, that this might be just God's way of testing the strength of our faith, and that we must prove that strength by fighting with more confidence than ever in Him? Do you remember that, Simon?"

Simon nodded, raising his head a little.

"Yes, Rabbi. I do."

"You do. Fine! But it seems something has happened since then to—weaken this great faith of yours in our Father in heaven. What was it? The Romans went far beyond Kabul, didn't they? They took even Jerusalem, the seat of our holy temples, and now they have wrested from us our very last stronghold, Bethar. Little Judea lies writhing once again under the boot of imperial Rome. Pitiful sight! And what does all this prove, my son? Why, that God may very well be elsewhere while his people suffers and perishes, doesn't it?"

"No, no, it doesn't!" Simon burst out. He sat down heavily and leaned forward, holding his head in his hands.

Akiba remained standing, looking down at him.

"I'm glad to hear you say that. Then why, do you think, has God permitted all this to happen?"

Simon met his eyes again.

"Because I—I am not a true Messiah. God exists, and is deeply concerned about our misfortunes, but I am not His true Messiah!"

"And His Voice coming to you in the street on your way to me—"

"It was not His Voice! I only imagined it! I *dreamed* it!"

Akiba paused.

"You forget, my son, that I heard it too—the very next day. Do you think we are *both* fools?"

"Then if I am a true Messiah, why are we here? How is it we haven't been able to protect Bethar? Why were the Romans able to slaughter their way back into our country?"

"You are asking difficult questions, Simon. I can try to answer them, but, though I am a Rabbi, I am nothing more than a human being, just like yourself, and can therefore only use whatever wisdom God has given me to understand Him and His ways. Why, you demand, has He sent you to deliver us and then allowed us to go down in defeat? But are you sure—*very* sure, Simon—that we *are* defeated?"

"What do you mean?"

"The Romans have also suffered huge losses. I do not know—perhaps only God knows—what Hadrian is thinking at this moment. If God but wills it, He can make him deeply regret this whole campaign and resolve, should another revolt break out, to let Judea go its own way and worship Him in peace. If this should happen, it will be our revolt which will be honored and remembered for having prepared the way for it. Don't you see that?"

"In other words, other Jewish leaders—rabbis and statesmen of the future—will look back to us for a kind of . . . inspiration, so that our efforts will not have been in vain."

"Yes!" the Rabbi exclaimed proudly. "You *do* see, don't you?"

"I do, Rabbi. Still . . ."

"What?"

"My wife Leah. My son Rufus. I'll never see them again!"

"Yes, your wife and son—I remember them very well."

"And your wife too! Rachel."

"My dear Rachel. True. But Simon, we must remember we are soldiers. So many Jewish families have already lost husbands and fathers. When we faced the enemy, we knew it might mean farewell to the ones we loved the most." He sat down beside him and put his arm around him. "We should pray now, Simon, for God's will still rules the world, and we must be humble enough to accept it."

And so they prayed until their half hour was up, and the guard returned and led the Rabbi to another room.

The day passed quickly, and Simon knew it would not be long before they would be taken out to be executed. He called to his guard, "Soldier!"

The Roman approached suspiciously, his hand firmly on his sword, for it had been made clear to him that if this valuable prisoner were allowed to escape, his own life would be forfeit.

"What is it?"

"May I have a bit of scroll?"

"Scroll?"

"Yes. I wish to write a letter to my—my family."

The guard grinned.

"What makes you think they will get it?"

Simon spoke in a tone of abrupt command, exactly as if he were still leading a revolt of hundreds of thousands of men:

"Tell Julius Severus I want to talk to him again!"

"Yes, sir!" he replied quickly, and immediately raced off with the message. It was only when he was already halfway to Julius's quarters that he realized there was really no reason for such haste. He shook his head and slowed up a little. What a forceful man that was! One could hardly think of him as a prisoner at all, with just a few hours to live.

Julius was surprised and a little annoyed.

"What does he want to see me about?" he asked.

"He—he said he wants to write a letter to his family. He needs a scroll."

"Give it to him," he shrugged, and then stirred from his comfortable chair. "Wait—I'll see him myself."

In a few minutes he entered Simon's room, two guards escorting him. The prisoner glanced at this stalwart support and could not help smiling.

"Afraid of me, Julius?"

"There's no reason why you shouldn't attack me, Simon. We are still enemies, and a soldier is always wise to take precautions."

"You are right. I—I hope I haven't disturbed you."

"No, you haven't. Tinnius, Publius and I have been adding up our losses. They have been very great—far greater than we ever expected in dealing with so small a people as yours."

"Small, Julius? In the eyes of our God, every human being is large."

"Yes, your God. I think I have heard enough of Him. Tell me, Simon—you wish to write your family?"

"Yes, my wife and son."

"Ah! You have a son too."

"Yes, Rufus. A wonderful boy. Would you give me the courtesy of delivering my message to them? They are both in Jerusalem." As the other hesitated, he went on a little warmly, "Surely you would not deny a soldier his—"

Julius raised his hand.

"Agreed. You have been a bold and dangerous opponent, and as another soldier I respect you for it. You shall have your scroll." He turned to one of the guards and ordered, "Give him whatever writing materials he asks for." He faced Simon again. "Your family will hear from you—you have my word on it."

"Thank you, Julius."

The Roman wheeled and left. The guards followed, one of them locking the room.

Soon the prisoner was writing Leah and Rufus the very last letter they were to receive from him:

"My dear Leah and Rufus,

Julius Severus has promised to deliver this to you, and

so I feel I am not writing these lines in vain. No doubt you have heard by this time of the fate of Bethar and its gallant soldiers. Rabbi Akiba is here with me now—his room is not far from mine—and we are both to meet God within a few hours. But I am sad only because I shall not see either of you again in this life. In other ways I am happy—I feel we have dealt the Romans a blow which they will feel for many generations to come, and which the Jews will always remember too. You, Rufus! When you grow up to be a man, you will understand many things which I cannot explain now, and one of these will be what Jews must take a stand for, or they perish—the right to be themselves, to worship their God just as their forefathers did, to be true to their sacred traditions. For we are not animals, but men, and as such we must pass on to our children what we have learned from our own fathers—especially what is most precious and holy and should last forever."

He stopped for a few moments, remembering the brave face Rufus had made when they had last parted. Then he went on:

"Be of good courage, my son, as I know you will be. Do not forget me and what our fine soldiers have tried to accomplish. And you, Leah—you must now take my place and make sure Rufus grows to manhood as strong as he would have been if I had been there to help him. God bless and keep you both!"

He laid his pen down on the table, leaned back and closed his eyes. There was little more he could say. How he longed to see them both once again, even if it were for just a single moment!

Next morning, together with Rabbi Akiba, he was put to death by the sword. They died calmly, praising God.